RISE OF THE ULTRAS

THE LAST HERO, BOOK 2

MATT BLAKE

MATTBLAKEAUTHOR.COM

If you want to be notified when Matt Blake's next novel is released, please sign up to his mailing list.

http://mattblakeauthor.com/newsletter

Your email address will never be shared and you can unsubscribe at any time.

Cameron Doyle rushed down the corridor towards Area 64 and hoped to the Lord above that his worst fears weren't true.

The corridor was dark, which in itself was unusual. Usually, this tunnel that led right underneath the Mojave Desert for miles—ten, to be exact—was lit with an ambient hue, which always reminded Cameron of a hospital ward. That ambience always came with a hum, too, the only thing cutting through the silence in the total quiet of the desert. He knew there was nothing above him, no cars driving over, no people walking past. And even if there were, he wouldn't be able to hear them.

But just the sheer knowledge that he was completely alone not just down here, but above... it gave him the shivers.

Now there was no light but the torch on his mobile phone, and there was no hum of the ambient lights, Cameron Doyle felt more lonely than he'd ever felt down here before.

He could taste a bitter hint of sick in his mouth. It'd been something he'd suffered with for years. Acid reflux struck at two times—first thing in the morning, without fail. And whenever he was nervous, without fail.

It was first thing in the morning.

And he was terrified.

There was a metallic smell to the air the further he got down the tunnel, which merged with the smell of his sweat. There was supposed to be air con down here, but that had malfunctioned too. Lights, air conditioning... he just had to pray not *everything* had malfunctioned. Because if everything had malfunctioned, that'd mean...

No. He couldn't think about what it'd mean if everything malfunctioned. There were measures in place. Safety measures. Backup generators to the backup generators. He knew, deep down, that he should've pushed harder for a move towards embracing ULTRA powers to keep this place running. ULTRA power was infinite, but they were still trying to harness it without a living being behind it.

They were getting there. There were experiments—experiments that went way out of his comfort zone.

But soon enough, like everything in the world, they'd get there.

He just hoped it wasn't too late.

He felt his heart racing and his chest tightening the closer he got to the Area 64 main entrance. Usually, he simply had to stand on a moving walkway, which raced him over to the other side in a matter of seconds. He wasn't exactly overweight, but he wasn't all that fit either. He spent most of his time underground, and he didn't have a family to go home to—unless his elderly mother counted as family. He liked to kick back and watch documentaries on Netflix when he wasn't down here, underground. Basically, he didn't move around a lot. He didn't need to.

And he was cool with that.

He felt the walls closing in, and he knew he was close. Part of him just wanted to turn around and run away. Because he didn't want to be the one to discover the bad news. He didn't want to be the one to tell Mr. Parsons what had happened. Mr. Parsons wasn't exactly the forgiving type.

Besides, he didn't want to be responsible for the mass of destruction that would occur if his deepest fears were realized.

He picked up his pace regardless as the walls narrowed some more. In the dim light of his phone torch, he saw a flash of steel, and he recognized the door. A door he'd been through so many times, that he'd felt nervous about going through so many times.

But never like he felt right now. Never anything like this.

He slowed down as he approached it. Listened to the perfect silence. Very few people actually worked down here— the security of this area was completely digitized apart from his occasional visits to gather research, check everything was in order. After all, mere humans couldn't do a thing to protect this place. Nobody could do a thing to protect this place.

They had fail-safes, of course. Fail-safes in case of disasters. But much like the fail-safes when developing a nuclear device or a particle accelerator, the fail-safes weren't really rooted in reality. They were just there to make the governments feel better, more secure, about their pursuit of power.

There were no fail-safes that would be able to control what was through this door.

There was no power like what was behind this door.

Cameron lifted his shaking hand. He pressed it against the palm reader.

Nothing happened.

For a moment, he didn't know what was occurring. The palm reading was just the first step in a long series of security measures to get through this door. Palms could be replicated, but reading out a favorite passage from a favorite novel in your exact intonation? Remembering nineteen 18-character passwords and inputting them with the exact sequence of fingers? That wasn't quite as easy.

But the palm reading was the first step. And that wasn't even working.

Cameron stood still for a few seconds until it dawned on him. Of course the palm reader wasn't working. If the power were out, so too would this...

But wait. No. The security system was based elsewhere in the event of a problem like this. Somewhere off the coast of Alaska, remotely powered through tiny wires trailing through the surface of the earth. If anything came within a mile of those underground wires, it'd be fried before it had the chance to explain itself.

And yet here Cameron was, standing in front of the door, the palm reader not working.

He lifted his phone. There wasn't any signal down here, but he had an emergency line where he'd have to report his findings. He lifted it to his ear, dreading breaking the news. He'd have to call it. Someone would have to call it.

And then he noticed something.

There was a slight glimmer of light along the side of the door.

He lowered his phone. Stepped closer to that light. Usually, this door was sound and light proof. But there was a trail alongside the right side. An uneven trail, like the door had been...

When Cameron put his hand on the door, just lightly, he got his answer.

The heavy metal door fell forward.

Crashed down onto the other side with deafening ferocity.

He tensed for a few seconds. Partly because of the sound of that crash, partly because he didn't want to face what was behind the door. He didn't want to see what was inside.

But eventually, he saw what was inside.

He saw *exactly* what was inside.

Or rather, he saw what wasn't inside.

The room was arranged much like a prison. Eight rows of cells, all leading down. Only these weren't just normal cells. These were cells designed to keep the strongest of forces inside. Unbreakable even to the power of thought.

All of the cell doors were open.

Cameron blinked a few times. He couldn't move a muscle. Eighteen cells on eight floors. That made one hundred and forty-four unaccountable for. One hundred and forty-four of the most powerful *things* in existence, locked up in this cell for... well, some of them for a long time.

All of them pissed.

Pissed at the world for trapping them in here.

Pissed at the world for—

Cameron felt the movement behind him before he heard it; before he saw it.

He didn't want to turn around. He didn't want to face whoever was there. He knew it'd be the last face he ever looked at.

But eventually, tears welling in his eyes, he accepted that turning and looking in that face was a far better fate than reporting a mass escape of imprisoned ULTRAs from the highest security prison on the planet.

He felt his teeth chattering. Took in as deep a breath as he could. This was his responsibility. This was on him. And he'd failed.

He turned around and looked the person—the *thing* —behind him in the eye.

When he saw what it was, his entire body froze.

He thought this was the good way out. He thought this was the better way to go.

But he was wrong.

He was so, so wrong.

He scrambled for his phone. Went to dial in HQ with his shaky fingers.

But then his fingers wouldn't move. They were locked. Completely locked.

And so too was the rest of his body.

"Don't worry," the deep voice said. Footsteps moved towards him. He felt a cold shiver cover his body, getting progressively worse by the second. "It'll be over soon."

He felt his body getting stiffer, harder, beyond the point he could move.

But as he stared the thing opposite in its eyes, he couldn't hide from his thoughts. He couldn't hide from the knowledge of what was coming.

The greatest storm of all was brewing.

And there was nothing his paralyzed body could do about it.

There was nothing anybody was going to be able to do about it.

Nothing, other than pray.

"**M**an, all the things we've been through and you're still afraid of some damned bears?"

I sat opposite the crackling campfire in the total darkness. Truth be told, I was a bit worried about bears, as much as Damon reassured me there were no bears in New York State, black bears aside. I'd read a story a while back that revealed the number of wild animals and escaped zoo animals hiding in the woods.

And sure. I could handle a wild animal if I really wanted to.

But I didn't really want to. I just wanted to be me, Kyle Peters. I just wanted to be a seventeen-year-old kid who camped with his friends and told stupid stories.

I wanted to be normal.

But of course, I wanted to save the world every now and then, too.

"I saw a documentary once," Avi said. "About this bear that hunted down these kids."

"Not sure I wanna hear this right now," Ellicia said.

Avi leaned in close to the fire. It lit up his face. Not literally.

"They sneaked away, all four of 'em. Ended up back home, back in the city. But the bear was onto their scent."

"I think I can see where this is going," I said.

"It sneaked into their home at night," Avi said, the excitement in his voice showing how much he was enjoying himself. "Unlocked the door with its big bear nails."

Ellicia giggled. Damon looked a little... well, he looked a little afraid, not gonna lie.

"And then it crept up the stairs. Walked into the first kid's bedroom. Leaned over with its mega sharp teeth, slavering all over, and it went... BOOM!"

Avi clapped his hands together and shouted that last word. It made Damon jump a bit, but me and Ellicia were totally still. Must've seen it coming from a mile away.

"Great story," I said. "How long did that one take you?"

"Hey," Avi said, stoking the fire. The heat of the flames was intense but nice in the biting cold of early December. Yeah, camping in December. Must be crazy. But we had plenty of sleeping bags, and Damon promised he'd huddle us all like penguins if it got too cold. "At least I have a few real stories of my own, bro. Not like you, fallin' to sleep in, I dunno, only the biggest news story of the last forever years."

I knew what Avi was referring to, and I felt my mind wandering as the smell of the burning wood filled my nostrils, blurred with those past memories. Half a year had passed since I'd embraced Glacies, my ULTRA identity, and taken down Nycto. Since that day, there'd been hunts for Glacies, but a sense of calm had set in. Most key figures thought he was dead. And anyway, people weren't fighting as much. The world seemed relieved again. Relieved to get another chance at living.

I hadn't exactly retired Glacies. There were times when I still used him. To fight crime. To stop assaults.

But I knew the truth of the life I was living now.

I had to keep my identity quiet. I had to keep Glacies out of the limelight.

Sure, I had people to look out for. But more important than that, I had a life as a seventeen-year-old to live. I had camping trips to go on.

Oh, and I had a girlfriend.

I felt Ellicia squeeze my hand. It still seemed surreal that stuff like this was happening to me, as we sat under the stars listening to Damon and Avi talk about the latest shows they were watching on streaming TV, as well as whether the next iPhone was gonna be as revolutionary as everyone was predicting.

"You okay?" I asked.

"Me okay? You look like you've seen a ghost."

I squeezed her hand back. "Just tired. And cold. And hungry. And—"

"Questioning why in the hell we're out here in mid-December?"

I smiled. "Something like that."

Of course, there were obvious reasons for me wanting to keep Glacies a secret. I had the ability to move at super speed, to teleport, to turn invisible. If I really concentrated, I could embrace super strength and fly. If I concentrated even harder, I could make weird ice-like stuff fire outta my hands, and heal myself. Again, a neat party trick, but not one I could go showing off in a world still hostile to ULTRAs despite all the good most of them had done. Myself included.

But there were other reasons I held off Glacies too. Not just because it was revealed that Nycto was Daniel Septer, a guy from our school, ramping the whole school paranoia up to the max. But because I was actually feeling better about myself, Kyle Peters. I felt more confident since I'd fought off Nycto; since I'd saved the world. And the strength Glacies gave me had seeped over into my normal life. It'd made me ask Ellicia out. It put me here, camping in the middle of December. It made me do things I never used to do when I was too much of a wuss to do them and say things I'd never say when people were putting me down.

Glacies was cool, sure. I owed everything to Glacies. Being Glacies had made me stronger. It'd made me believe in myself for the first time since my sister died over eight years ago in the Great Blast.

I was stronger because of Glacies, sure. But I had a life to live as Kyle Peters. I didn't *need* to be an ULTRA anymore to be strong in my own life.

But there were times when I needed to be an ULTRA for other reasons.

Almost on cue, I heard Damon swear. "Shit."

I saw the concern on his face. "Whatsup?"

Damon rubbed the back of his neck. "Some hostage situation down my street. Armed robbers inside a nightclub. Holding loadsa innocent people hostage."

I felt a wave of sickness cover me, a wave of duty charge through me. "What do they want?"

Damon shrugged. "I dunno. Looks like some kinda revenge job on the owner."

"But why should innocent people have to pay?" Ellicia said.

"They shouldn't," I muttered.

"Huh?"

I shook my head and zoned back in. "Nothing. I, um... I'm gonna go take a leak."

I squeezed Ellicia's hand again and then I stood up. Headed towards the pitch blackness of the trees.

"Don't get eaten by a bear!" Damon called.

"I'll try not to. But if you don't hear from me... well, you're just gonna have to come looking for me."

"Screw that," Avi said.

I smiled. That was exactly what I wanted to hear.

I'd be a little longer. They'd think I was messing around. Eventually, I'd give up and go back to join them.

Yeah. That's what I wanted them to believe. What they had to believe.

Of course, I was doing something completely different.

I stood behind a tree and looked up at the jet black night sky. I could hear the city in the distance.

I held my breath, focused on everything that made me mad, focused on the people I'd lost, the screams I'd heard, and then I shot myself back into my bedroom. The teleportation had been hard to master at first, but it was getting more seamless. It was like using any muscle. I had to keep practicing. Had to keep perfecting what I was doing.

It was the only way I could keep people safe.

I hovered just off the floor of my bedroom, being careful not to make any creaks on the floorboards. Mom and Dad were watching television downstairs. I didn't want to scare them. Learning they had an ULTRA son might just put them in hospital for good. They'd never forgiven the ULTRAs for what happened to my sister, Cassie. Even though Orion sacrificed himself to save the world—even though *I'd* saved their lives as Glacies—still they hadn't found it in their hearts to see the good in ULTRAs.

It was cool. Something I just had to live with.

Another reason I couldn't be Glacies full time.

Just when I had to be.

I looked over the chest of drawers in front of me. Opened it with a key I kept on me at all times. I turned the lock, and then I turned the lock of the next box in there. Once I was in there, I focused on the tight wooden casing, pouring all the strength into my hands. It was so tight that I couldn't open it with my bare hands. No one could.

But I was an ULTRA. So things were different.

The casing opened up, and I saw it.

The black mask. The tight black outfit. The eagle on the middle of the chest embossed onto it as an unforgettable logo.

I lifted up the outfit and felt pride surge through me. Pride and fear. Pride at the people Glacies had saved, but fear at the risk I took every time I embraced Glacies.

The risk of being exposed.

The risk of being killed.

The risk of throwing away my life as Kyle Peters for life as an ULTRA, hunted, condemned.

I thought about teleporting back to upstate, going back to camping. I thought about leaving all this behind because the police would handle it. Someone else would deal with it.

But then I remembered all the fear I'd felt when I was caught up in that gunman situation back in the stadium, feeling totally afraid, totally defenseless, and I knew I couldn't let anyone in that nightclub feel the same way for any longer.

I lifted my Glacies outfit.

Put it on.

I had work to do.

I stood outside the nightclub on Richmond Terrace and waited to strike.

The situation inside there was just as Damon had described it. There were gunmen, at least five of them, all dressed in black, all holding long rifles and pointing them to the heads of customers, who were on their knees. I saw the look of fear in the eyes of suited men. I saw tears streaming down the faces of girls in their early twenties, not much older than me. They were innocent in this. Whatever had happened for these gunmen to attack this club, those people in there had no part in it, so there was no sympathy for the gunmen from me.

I held my breath and kept my camouflage strong. There was a weird, eerie silence about the street. People walked by but kept their distance. There were signs of police, but they weren't stepping inside, instead trying to negotiate with the captors.

I knew they might have a shot at coming to an agreement. But sometimes in this world, people didn't want to come to agreements.

They just wanted to prove a point.

I smelled burning somewhere, and it reminded me of Ellicia, Damon, and Avi. They'd be camping upstate, in front of that crackling fire. I knew right now they'd be getting concerned about me, convinced I was playing some kind of trick. Maybe they'd be searching for me—if they could conquer their fear of bears to do so.

Whatever they were doing, wherever they were, I was Glacies right now.

I had a job to do.

And I had to do it fast.

"We'll end this *all* right here, sunshine," one of the gunmen said in a southern drawl. He had his rifle to a blonde woman's head. I could hear her teeth shaking from here. "You just tell me where Casey Clyne is. Then we'll let you go."

"I don't know," the woman sniveled, and I realized then from her black outfit that she worked here. She was a bartender, or hostess or something. Casey Clyne must be the guy who owned the place. The guy these gunmen had issues with.

The gunman shook his head. "You know, when you're on your knees like this, peeing your pants, you're supposed to wanna do anything to help a guy like me out. Ain't that right, crew?"

"Yessir," a couple of the men muttered.

"Police," I heard the loudspeaker crackle. "Lower your weapons and step out with your hands above your head. Do *not* make us fire."

The main guy laughed. "Like they're gonna send a spray of bullets through the windows and risk you lovely people," he said. "Nah. Nah, they got this wrong. They got this wrong 'cause I don't negotiate. Ain't that right, boys?"

"Yessir."

"Yessir. And now it's time. Time to ask you kindly one final time. Where's Casey Clyne hidin', princess?"

The woman squeezed her eyes together. Her head lowered further towards the floor. "I—I swear. I swear I—I don't—I don't... Please."

The masked man tilted his head to one side.

"Well, that's just too darned bad."

He lifted the rifle.

Pressed it to the back of the woman's head.

Squeezed the trigger.

The gun shot out of his hands before the bullet could pierce through that woman's skull.

I kicked it away. And then I punched the man in the neck, right in his Adam's apple.

I held my breath and kept my camouflage, moving on to the next four men. I could see some of them looking around, confused.

I had to be quick. I had to act fast.

I kicked the next guy in the shins. Sent him flying back into his friend, knocking the pair of them down like dominos.

I kept on fighting, determined for nobody to see me as Glacies. I couldn't give up my disguise. I had to have everyone believe the last moment I'd been alive was when I'd disappeared into Krakatoa with Nycto, buried him in the lava.

Otherwise, they'd be onto me. Whether I'd done good or bad, they'd be onto me.

I couldn't let that happen.

The fourth man lifted his rifle and fired in my direction.

I dodged the bullet. Jumped around him. Appeared at the other side and smacked him in the back of his neck.

When he was down, I lifted the final hostage off the floor, keeping my camo as active as I could.

"Casey Clyne," I said. "Where the hell *do* I find him?"

The guy, again clearly someone who worked here, shook his

head as he tried to see where my words were coming from. "He's—I don't—"

"I don't know what your boss has done to get into this mess. Frankly, I don't care. But if you don't tell me where he is, I can't promise I'll be able to keep him safe—"

I heard gunshots from the stairs opposite. I pushed the man out of the way and saw two more masked men coming down the stairs. I focused on them. Felt the anger at them holding innocent people hostage.

I flew right into the path of the bullets, dodging them as well as I could.

Right into the chest of the first guy.

I knocked him down. Sent him crashing to the stairs.

And then I heard a shot and felt an agonizing burning sensation in my shoulder.

I looked up at the guy. I knew I was still camouflaged, but he was staring at me like I was *there*. So for that reason, I couldn't let him leave this place.

"You shouldn't've done that," I said.

I punched him hard in the stomach.

Held my breath.

I split through time and space.

The next thing I knew, I was standing in the icy cold, snowy mountains of Tibet.

The man looked around, teeth chattering, so out of place with his black mask, with his gun in hand.

"You'll find your way off this mountain," I said. "Eventually."

And then I bolted myself back to that club in New York.

When I got there, I was on the top floor. I knew I needed to check this place was safe. I had a bad feeling there'd be more hostages in here. Plus, there was Casey Clyne. Sure, he didn't sound an angel, but whoever he was, he couldn't be worse than the people threatening to kill his customers.

I rushed down the corridor, checking each and every door. Kept on going, eager to find more people to help, eager to catch the people responsible for this.

A door creaked behind me. I could feel someone focusing on my footsteps as my camouflage wavered. The bullet wound was hurting like hell, but I'd have to deal with it later. I turned around. Saw a man pointing a little pistol right at me.

He was short and plump, with a balding head and a white shirt drenched in sweat. I didn't even have to ask him to know he was Casey Clyne.

"Casey?" I said anyway.

He looked around, unsure of where the voice came from. "P-please. I'll pay you. I'll pay you as soon as I—"

I shifted behind him and grabbed him. "Don't turn around. When you've closed this place down, you're gonna pack your bags and you're never gonna show your face in New York City again."

"But—"

"If you value the safety of your customers, you'll close this place down right now. If you value your own safety, you'll—"

"Police! Hands in the air!"

I heard the footsteps running down the corridor. I tried to push for my camo, but the bullet wound in my shoulder was stinging. I could only focus on one thing at a time. And right now, I couldn't be seen.

I tried to teleport away. Tried to shift somewhere with Casey.

But I wasn't strong enough to carry another person with me.

"The police," Casey said. "I—I got set up. I got set up bad. They'll throw me inside, and they'll leave me to rot."

"Hands in the air!"

I heard doors kicking in. I saw that my camo had fully deactivated. The police were going to see me. They were going to know that Glacies was still alive.

I had to leave this place.

"Please. I got a kid. I can't just leave. Please."

I felt the guilt inside at knowing what I had to do. Mighta been an ULTRA—and a damned powerful one at that—but when I was wounded, I had my limitations.

And I had Kyle Peters under this suit, too.

I had the life of a seventeen-year-old to live.

"I'm sorry," I said. "Just... just try and get outta here."

"Please don't—!"

The police stepped around the door.

But it was already too late. I was gone.

I WALKED BACK through the trees towards the crackling fire. Damon, Ellicia, and Avi were still sat around.

I felt guilty for having to leave Casey behind. Sure, he was probably an asshole. But he was worried about someone. He had a kid. He was gonna end up in prison for something he didn't believe he'd done.

I'd walked away because I didn't want anyone to know that Glacies was still alive.

I'd walked away because I wanted to be Glacies when it suited me—and only when it suited me.

'Cause I had a life to live.

I twisted my shoulder. It was fine now. Bit of a sting, but fine as it could be.

"Boo," I said, as I approached my friends.

The three of them glanced over. They were playing cards.

"Nice try, asshole," Damon said. "I've seen scarier bears in the kids section at Target."

I sat down by Ellicia's side and picked up my hand of cards.

My friends still thought I was a weak-ass—a weak-ass who'd just failed at scaring them in the woods.

And I was cool with that.

4

"Pass me the spanner."

I handed Dad the thing that looked most spanner-like to me.

"That's not a spanner."

"How am I supposed to know what a spanner looks like?"

Dad scoffed, in disbelief. "Kyle, *everyone* knows what a spanner looks like."

I was in Peters' Parts. Again. Seemed like I spent my entire life in here these days. Since the confrontation between Glacies and Nycto, a lot of people around the world had found a new purpose in life. Just like the end of the last Era of the ULTRAs, people were learning to take advantage of life. To start at new hobbies, to pick up dropped dreams.

If you'd told me my dad would be one of those people, I'd never have believed you.

But weirdly, he was. He actually had turned over a leaf.

I watched Dad disappear under the car. We'd been working on an old red Ford Escort for a couple of months now. Classic car, real neat looking. I didn't tell Dad I'd nearly destroyed it when I was training my ULTRA abilities, of course. There'd have been a hell of a bigger cleanup job to work on.

In truth, I kind of wished I was destroying things, though. If there was one thing I was sure about in my life of many uncertainties, it was that I wasn't quite cut out for a job in the car repair industry.

I mean, hell. I didn't know what a spanner looked like. Doesn't that tell you something?

I listened to my dad whistling away while he worked under the car. I walked around the garage, which smelled like rusty metal and oil. There always used to be a dustiness to this place, a dampness lingering in the air since it closed down. But Dad had been working at getting it up to scratch all over again. He wasn't quite ready for opening again, he said. But he wanted me to help him fix up this red Escort so it was in working shape. Truth be told, I didn't believe it was possible. The thing didn't look functional. But then, what did I know about fixing cars?

And I didn't want to disrupt my dad. He'd been positive lately. Way more positive than I'd ever seen him.

"To think how different all this could've been," he mumbled.

I looked around. He was still under the car. "What d'you mean?"

"Well, Nycto. If he'd got his way. We wouldn't be in here right now. Working together. Or... well, you watching me work, anyway."

"Is that a good thing or a bad thing?"

Dad rolled from under the car and glared in my direction. I raised my hands and smiled, showed I was only joking. He slid back under again. I enjoyed the time with my dad, to be honest. Didn't enjoy working on a car, standing around like a lemon. But just seeing him with a sense of purpose in his life again. It made me feel good.

It made me feel less guilty about Cassie's death.

And it made me feel less like an ULTRA and more like a normal teenage kid.

"If Glacies hadn't stopped him then... hell, I dunno where we'd be right now."

I scratched the back of my neck. It was strange hearing my dad talk about Glacies in front of me. Kind of like he was chatting about someone he'd seen in the street without realizing they were a best friend of mine or something. Besides, he never spoke about the ULTRAs anyway. Neither of my parents did. They were still a sore spot for them after what happened to Cassie.

"We never really spoke," Dad continued, as if reading my mind.

"About what?"

"You know. The ULTRAs. The fight..."

He left it hanging there. And I swore I must be dreaming because Dad never, ever discussed this kind of thing.

"Well, what is there to say?" I asked.

He rolled back out from under the car. His hands were covered in oil, as were his blue overalls. "I dunno. I guess I'm saying I kinda respect Glacies. For what he did. The sacrifice he made."

He glanced at me just for a split second, but I felt something in that look. Something I couldn't explain. Something that made me feel uneasy.

"Yeah, well," I said, feeling my cheeks blush. "I feel a lot safer now both of those ULTRAs are long gone."

"Hmm," Dad said.

"Hmm, what?"

He shook his head. "Nothing."

"Go on, Dad. We never talk about this, like you said."

He stood by the side of the car wiping his hands. "It's just I keep thinking about Orion. About what he did. The Great Blast."

The taste in my mouth soured. Uh oh. I could see where this was going.

"Dad, we don't have to—"

"No," he said. "No, we do. I'm sick of dancing around the past like it never happened. What happened was horrible. Crazy. For so many people. So many lives lost. But after what happened with Glacies and Nycto, I guess I'm startin' to wonder whether Orion wasn't so bad after all. Whether he was... just tryin' to do the right thing. To take down Saint."

I felt stunned by my dad's admission. It was the first time he'd said anything of the kind in... well, ever.

"Maybe he was different after all," Dad said.

I thought about nodding. Thought about agreeing. In the end, I just cleared my throat and shook my head. "I'm not sure what to think."

Dad and I held eye contact for a while. I saw that glimmer in his eye again, that unplaceable look.

And then he looked away. "Anyway." He leaned into the car. Turned the key. Went to sit down, then stopped. "Actually, why don't you try starting her up?"

I gulped. "Me?"

"Well, you might as well seeing as she's about to be yours."

I stumbled when Dad said those words. Wasn't sure how to take them at first. "It's... it's mine?"

Dad smiled. He wiped his hands again, then patted me on the shoulder. "As soon as I get her fixed up completely, she's all yours. You're my boy, Kyle. And I'm proud of you. Way, way more than you realize."

He squeezed my shoulder, and I felt warmth fill my body as he looked me right in my eyes.

"You too, Dad," I said, a lump forming in my throat. "You too."

"Anyway, enough of the sappiness."

"Yeah. Sure." I stumbled into the car. Almost banged my head climbing in, which was a good start.

"She comfy?"

"She's... a car."

"Go on then. Start her up."

I turned the key and held my breath. And as I sat there in the car, beside my smiling, relatively healthy looking dad, it started to dawn on me that he was recovering. Finally, after over eight years of grief and pain, he was recovering from Cassie's death. He was returning to normality.

If my dad could go back to life how it was, if he could snap out of his sadness, then I knew I could be a normal seventeen-year-old.

With a healthy dose of sneaky Glacies related activities on the side, of course. Just not too many that they attract any attention.

I remembered the words of the Man in the Bowler Hat. That mysterious figure who'd stepped into my bedroom out of nowhere, given me a pep talk then vanished.

"You need to let Kyle die. You need to become somebody else entirely."

He'd made sense about some things. The things about believing in myself.

But I didn't believe him when he told me I had to kill one of my identities. I had to be careful, sure. I had to make sure I stayed on a low profile.

But I wasn't turning my back on anything in my life.

Because I was happy.

"Go on then!" Dad shouted.

I took in a deep breath.

Turned the key.

The car spluttered to life.

And as Dad and I celebrated, as the pair of us laughed and cheered together as my cool classic car came back to life, I had no idea that far, far away, something radical was happening.

Something that was going to change my life all over again.

Forever.

5

M r. Parsons looked around the emptied prison cells and felt sickness fill his body from head to toe.

This place was massive. But it was usually so full of life, even if that life was trapped behind the strongest metal doors. It housed some of the most dangerous ULTRAs the government had been able to track down over the years. After all, they couldn't just *kill* the ULTRAs they'd created. They had to use them. Use them for research. Try and find ways to retrain them so that they worked consistently in humanity's favor, and not against it.

But right now, every single cell door in Area 64 was open.

The ULTRAs were gone.

"What do you think we should do about it, sir?"

Mr. Parsons walked along the metal corridor past the open cell doors. Every single footstep echoed down through this vast chamber that usually housed so much power. The air was rich with the smell of burned metal. He wondered how this had happened—who had instigated the breakout. He had an idea, but that wasn't something he could worry about right now.

All he could worry about was how he was going to get the ULTRAs back.

How he was going to avert a national—international—crisis.

"I mean, one hundred and forty-four of them," Idris said in that pitiful little British accent of his. He was a short man with extremely round glasses perched on the end of his big, chunky nose. He never looked comfortable at the best of times, so you could imagine how he looked right now.

"I just don't understand how a thing like this can happen," Mr. Parsons said. He stopped by an open cell door. Looked inside it. He saw the bed erect in the middle of the room. Saw it propped up on that circular metal pole. He saw the bands where their arms were supposed to be chained down. The bright light above, that shone on and off intermittently throughout the day, so they could monitor each individual ULTRA's reaction to different stimuli.

"Main power down. Backup gens down. Backup to the backups—"

"Down," Mr. Parsons continued.

Idris blushed a little. He nodded, pushing his glasses back up his face. "So what do we do?"

Mr. Parsons looked around the vast expanse of Area 64. He'd been the one to come up with this place. During the last Era of the ULTRAs, when the figureheads of the governments wanted the ULTRAs banished from existence, he was the one to propose to the president that they didn't destroy the ULTRAs. Not entirely. Because they could come in handy one day.

The world of eight years ago wasn't ready for ULTRAs, or Heroes, as they then called them, but nobody dared utter now. Not just that, but the ULTRAs weren't ready for the world of eight years ago. It was a beta test gone horribly wrong. But they'd managed to get them under control, with the indirect assistance of an ULTRA called Orion. They'd managed to end the most immediate threats to existence.

And now, just like the Russians supposedly had samples of the smallpox virus hiding frozen in labs deep beneath the ground, America had a weapon of its own. An ultimate weapon that it was working on, refining to perfection, until the day came when the world would be ready for ULTRAs all over again.

But the fact of the matter stood.

The ULTRAs had escaped.

Someone had helped them escape.

"I mean, we can put out a warning," Idris said, scratching at his nose. "We—we can reach out to the news networks. Broadcast it globally. Tell people to stay in their homes. But that still leaves us with a lot of explaining to do."

Mr. Parsons looked over the balcony and waited a few seconds before responding. It was always his way. He was never one to interrupt. Never one to snap. He believed in always carefully considering what a person had to say, what their argument was. His temperament was a strong reason he'd managed to drag himself so far in the government's Secret Service, he believed.

He was renowned for his bold but successful decisions. His scary calls that, as terrifying as they sounded, always paid off. Always.

And as he saw the sequence of events paving out in front of him, he knew what he was going to have to do to end this chaos.

He knew what risk he was going to have to take.

Idris kept on mumbling away. "But I'm thinking we should just be honest and sincere. I'm thinking we should just go out there and tell the truth."

Mr. Parsons looked into Idris' eyes. He smiled. "We'll wake Project Ceta 453."

The glazed look that washed over Idris' face said it all. "But... but we can't—"

"I know it's not ideal," Mr. Parsons said, a rare moment of interruption to stop Idris getting in a frenzy. "I know it's not the perfect way to do things. And I know the project still has a lot of work to go."

"Too right it has a lot of work to go. We're risking a catastrophe here."

"And what other suggestions do you have?"

Idris' mouth hung open. The sheer time that passed told Mr. Parsons he didn't have an answer.

They only had once choice.

The pair of them walked out of Area 64 and made the long trip underground towards the next labs. The secret labs that required an even deeper level of security. The generators and power here were still running. They always would be.

But even if they weren't, this place didn't worry Mr. Parsons quite as much. Because he knew he had the capability to control what was inside it.

Mr. Parsons walked up to the door and went through the deep security measures, which took a whole fifteen minutes to pass. When he'd finished, he looked around and saw Idris standing there in a daze, just staring towards him.

"Are you okay, Idris?"

Idris snapped back into consciousness. He still looked glazed, though. Glazed and panicked. "It's just... I keep thinking."

"Thinking about what?"

"I thought it was over. This... this ULTRA business. I mean I knew we had them in captivity but I... I really never thought I'd see this day."

Mr. Parsons offered a half smile of understanding. Idris was weak. Very weak. If he weren't in the position of power he was in, working on some of the most secretive medical rescarch programs in world history, he'd not be fit for the new world.

Well, he probably wouldn't be fit for it anyway.

That much remained unclear.

After Idris had worked his way through security procedures of his own, he joined Mr. Parsons in walking through the door and inside the labs.

They passed scientists working in white coats on their way. Passed enormous screens, the sound of chatter filling the air in a way that completely contrasted Area 64.

He walked right to the back of the room. Leaned over Commander Browne's shoulder, as the commander sat staring through a thick glass window at something beyond.

"Activate Project Ceta 453," Mr Parsons said.

Commander Browne, a bulky man with a permanent frown on his face, peered around in amazement. "Are... are you sure?"

Mr. Parsons smiled. "Yes. It's our only option right now."

"But—"

"I understand your concerns. But it's all we've got left. So activate it. Please."

Commander Browne's reaction echoed that of Idris' earlier. Open mouthed amazement followed by closed mouth accep-tance. After all, he couldn't reject Mr. Parsons' request. He was his boss.

Commander Browne shouted commands down his micro-phone. The room erupted to life with the tapping of keyboards, the rush of adrenaline. All Mr. Parsons could do was look through that window of glass in front of him. That huge window into the future.

"They're scary bastards, huh?" Commander Browne asked.

Mr. Parsons kept on staring through the glass. Staring at the masses of people strapped to beds. Hundreds of them, all pinned down, all eyes closed.

"And they're absolutely ready to go?" Idris asked.

"Tests indicate so," Commander Browne said. "No minds of

their own. No focus of their own. Complete blank canvases that can't be changed. Speaking of which... what's our target? Because that's what we have to implant right now, and what we need to get rollin' for the next batch."

Mr. Parsons smiled at his army of ULTRAbots. Artificial creations with the abilities of ULTRAs, only completely controllable by humans. Not weapons that could grow to have a mind of their own, but mechanical weapons themselves. The perfect next step. The ideal evolution.

"Our target is the ULTRAs," Mr. Parsons said. "Every last one of them."

A pause. Then a few clicks of keys.

"And you're totally sure you wanna go ahead with this?" Commander Browne asked.

"The consequences of sitting back are far greater than leaving the ULTRAs to roam."

Commander Browne nodded. He hovered his finger over the return key. "Then we'll initiate the awakening."

A huge hiss of steam filled the room behind the glass. It completely covered up that army of ULTRAbots, completely whitened the room. And as Mr. Parsons waited, the entire room watched with quietened anticipation. With adrenaline.

This was the only option.

This was all he could do. All anyone could do.

The room was totally quiet, totally silent, for another few minutes.

And then an ULTRAbot flew at the glass and stared, red-eyed, right through at the labs, before shooting up through the roof, out into its new world.

The ULTRAs' days were numbered.

Whether they'd escaped Area 64 or were still out there for whatever reason, hiding, their time was coming to an end.

A new era had arrived.

6

"I 've got the squirts, sir! Sir, I've got the squirts!"

Okay, a quick recap. I might have ULTRA abilities, I might have the girl of my dreams, I might have more confidence and a hell of a happier life now than I did before I'd discovered my powers.

But when you were at school, did that make you immune to being remembered for your past?

No. Did it hell.

I walked past the two freshmen and tried to smile as they did an impression of me. Yes, I might've been Glacies. I might've saved the planet. But to them, I was just the guy who ran away from the end of semester football game to shit himself.

Even though I technically *didn't* shit myself. Not literally, anyway. Fake-shit. That's what my friends called it. In fact, that term had been coined since for people making excuses. *"You're just fake-shitting!"*

I was kinda proud. Kinda.

Just a pity these guys didn't know me for my real heroics.

"Seriously don't think anyone's ever gonna let that fake-shit thing die," Damon said, as we walked from Art class towards the yard. It was cold and icy out, New York in the grasps of a long winter. There hadn't been much snow yet, but apparently a big storm was on its way. I was pleased about that. Always loved snow days. We had just over a week to go at school before we finished for the Christmas break, too, so right now was a pretty good time to be alive.

"Sure it won't be that big a deal in a few months."

"You said that like a week after it happened. Kids who never even know what happened are comin' up to you and sayin' it."

I looked back. Saw those two freshmen still doing an impression of me, laughing away to each other. "Yeah, well. I guess Mike Beacon's memory's living on in a weird kinda way."

We didn't speak much about Mike Beacon or the other victims of the end-of-year-party attack. No one did. It was one of those scars was still extra sore. Mike might've been a douchebag to me, but he was a hero to the rest of the school. They'd built a memorial garden over by the tennis courts, but students tended to avoid it. It was weird, in a way. Reminded us of our own mortality, which wasn't something you wanted to be reminded of when you were only seventeen.

Those deaths were a scab that nobody wanted to pick. A reminder of what ULTRAs could do, the chaos they could cause if they really wanted to.

A reminder that a world with ULTRAs would never be safe.

"Still gets to me," Damon said.

I looked at him. He wasn't looking directly at me. But he was speaking serious, which wasn't like Damon at all. "What does?"

"The whole party thing. How it coulda... Man, you're the luckiest dude in the world that you weren't in that place when it got attacked. Where I was, in the middle of the floor. It was like hell opened up."

I was immediately transported back to the moment I'd saved Damon and Ellicia from the smoke and the flames inside that party venue. If only Damon knew what I'd done for him, what I'd seen, all the things I'd seen.

"Anyway. Looks like I'm gonna get stolen off you in three, two…"

I didn't know what Damon was on about until I saw Ellicia walking towards me. I found that weird. Ellicia and I didn't hang around much at school, even if we were together. We decided we'd keep within our friendship groups. We'd seen so many friendships split apart by relationships that we didn't want to risk the same happening to us, not with friendships as strong as we had. Besides, we hung out a lot outside school anyway.

So it was weird seeing her walk towards me on her own.

"Hey," she said. She didn't look right in my eyes, but I could tell she was upset about something. "Can we talk?"

She glanced at Damon, and I knew what she was hinting at right away. "Sure. Damon, do you, um…"

Damon raised his hands. "Hey. Whatever you got to say, you can say it in front of…"

Ellicia glared at Damon.

"Okay, okay. I'll meet you in the yard in five. Be there or be… well, the same shape, but slightly lower in my estimations."

He punched me on the arm and disappeared around the side of the school.

"You okay?" I asked.

Ellicia nodded. And then she shook her head. I was convinced right then that something had happened with her friends. It wasn't common, but girls did seem to argue over fickle things a hell of a lot more than boys. "Kyle, I… there's something I've been meaning to tell you."

I felt the dread building up right then. Saw a million

scenarios in my mind. She was ill? She'd kissed some other guy? She was, heaven forbid, *breaking up* with me?

But the answer was far worse than I could imagine.

"My parents. They're moving. We're all moving."

I narrowed my eyes. My cheeks heated up. I rubbed the back of my neck. "That's... Moving where?"

From the upset tone in her voice, I figured she wasn't just moving down the street.

"Ellicia? Where?"

"Arizona," she said.

"Ariz..." I nearly collapsed right there on the spot. "But that's... that's, like, miles away. Lots of miles."

Ellicia nodded. "My dad. He got a new job. They didn't give him long to start so we're gonna have to get packing soon."

"Soon? How soon is soon?"

"Three weeks."

"Three..."

I looked away. I couldn't speak anymore. Couldn't say anything. I didn't want to make a fool of myself. Besides, getting upset only triggered those powers inside me that I knew I didn't want to emerge right now.

"I like what we've got. And I still wanna see you."

"But you're gonna be the other side of the country."

"We can Skype," Ellicia said.

She smiled, and I wished I could've shared her enthusiasm, but I knew what was happening right here. I wasn't stupid. "You're breaking up with me."

"Well, it'll be hard, but... Kyle, I'm sorry."

"What about Columbia?"

"Well hopefully I'll still go there. But that's still some time away."

"Time to find someone new to change your plans."

"What?"

"Nothing. Nothing."

Ellicia reached her hand out. Touched my arm. Instead of it making me feel warm like it usually did, I felt cold. Cold all over. "I'm sorry, Kyle. I really... I really like you. But it's just the way things go sometimes."

I nodded. Kept my focus away from Ellicia. I resisted the tingling sensations in my body which pulled at me to teleport myself away from here. Far, far away.

"We've still got three weeks. We should... we should hang out. Until then."

"What's the point?"

I didn't mean to say it with such venom. I felt like an idiot right away. But I saw the bloodshot look in Ellicia's eyes and I knew the damage had already been done.

"Ellicia, I'm..."

She pulled her hand away and turned around. Started to walk away.

I wanted to fight for her. Hell, I wanted to tell her I could go visit her using my ULTRA abilities whenever I wanted. But that would just bring problems. There were only so many times I could explain to her how I'd afforded the flight, only so many times I could avoid my friends and family figuring out my secret.

My only option would be to watch her while she was alone.

And that wasn't right. That was just... creepy.

I wanted to fight for the girl I loved.

Instead, I watched her walk away, and I stood alone.

I DIDN'T SEE them watching from the opposite side of the school.

Watching very closely.

7

I wasn't usually the kind of guy who got pulled back in for detentions. But I figured after the love of my damned life just told me she was moving to Arizona in three weeks, a bit of slacking at school was just about justified.

I sat staring at the blank sheet of paper in front of me. I was supposed to be writing lines, but hell knew what Mrs. Porter asked me to write. Something about not curling up in a ball on the table and sobbing in class. Something about not shouting back at a teacher. Something about not storming out and making a scene.

Yeah. I'd made a bit of an ass of myself. But again, I figured I was well within my rights.

I looked up as I sat alone at the desk. Mrs. Porter was at the front of the class marking papers. I thought about asking her what lines she wanted me to write again, but knowing the way she was with me—and with everyone for that matter—it'd just further convince her to add an extra thousand, or something.

Funny really, the idea of lines. Do they actually work? What's the point of etching those same words in, over and over? "I WILL HAND IN MY WORK ON TIME. I WILL NOT

BE A DOUCHEYMCDOUCHEBAG." Was that kind of medieval brainwashing even effective at all? I could be at home right now doing something productive with my life. Like actual work. Or actual douchey-mc-douchebaggery.

Or lying in bed and sulking about Ellicia breaking up with me. Yeah, that was more believable.

The class was silent. So too was the entire campus. I looked at my watch. Half five. I'd been here forty-five minutes just waiting for Mrs. Porter to tell me what she wanted me to do. I'd seen other students in detention finish up their punishments and leave way before me. I figured there must be some kind of law about this. Student rights, or something.

What was stopping me standing up and leaving this place?

What was stopping me transporting Mrs. Porter to the other side of the world and leaving her in the middle of the Gobi Desert?

I smirked at the thought. Probably the first time I'd smirked all afternoon.

"Something funny, Mr. Peters?"

I sighed. Trust her to catch the one time I slip up. Trust her. "No. Not really."

"Not really?"

"It's just..." I shook my head.

"No. Go on. You've started now. You can finish."

I leaned back and figured I'd let it all out. After all, what else did I have to lose? "It's this. These... these *stupid* lines. I mean, what's the point? What am I actually learning here?"

Mrs. Porter glared at me, her expression unwavering.

"My girlfriend split up with me. Moving to Arizona in three weeks. Traveling to the other side of the *damned* world—"

"Not technically."

"Yeah, well, just allow me this right now. She's traveling miles away. And I'm not gonna see her again. Not... not like now. So there. That's why I slipped up in class. That's why I made a d... an idiot of myself. And I'm sorry, but right now I just wish I was back home so I could figure this stuff out."

Mrs. Porter was silent for a few moments. I could practically hear the clockwork ticking away in her brain, trying to figure out how to best punish me for my outburst.

Weirdly, she didn't punish me at all.

She closed her book, lowered her glasses and half-smiled.

"Young love is fickle. You'll get over it. On your way."

I couldn't believe what I'd just heard. Mrs. Porter, the biggest demon in this entire school, was letting me leave.

"Did I hear you right?"

"Kyle, I'm not the monster you think I am. I'm just doing my job, contrary to what you might think. Now go on. Shoot off. I've got a life to live too. And don't break down in class again. Please. If you're having trouble, you know where I am."

That half-smile of hers actually became a smile.

I looked at the palms of my hands to check the lines hadn't moved. This had to be some kind of weird dream.

I stood up. Gathered my bags and walked out of class. Every step I took to the door, I was convinced Mrs. Porter was going to stop me, call me back. That she'd just been pretending all along, and actually she wanted me to write out another nine-hundred pages of lines. I WILL NOT BREAK DOWN IN TEARS IN DEMON PORTER'S CLASS.

But she didn't.

I left her class and walked down the corridor.

After hours, school always felt weird. Totally quiet, but if you focused enough, you could still sense the echoes of the students who'd pushed their way down the corridor in the days, who'd tripped on their laces and fallen down the stairs. But right now, it felt creepier than ever. More quiet than ever. It was dark outside. The fluorescent lights beamed down from above. As I walked past each and every empty classroom, I couldn't shake the feeling that someone was watching me.

I hopped down the stairs and kept my head down. Tried not to look inside the classrooms at the empty chairs, at the teachers' seats, vacant, like some kind of weird old reconstruction museum. I felt a twinge of sickness in my stomach. A sudden urge to get out of this place. Like my body was telling me something was wrong.

Like Glacies was telling me something was wrong.

I walked over to the door and lowered the handle.

The door didn't budge.

I froze for a few seconds. I could see the first specks of snow falling in the darkness outside. I went to turn the handle again. It sometimes got a bit sticky in winter.

But it wasn't moving.

The door was locked.

Dread filled my body. The janitor must've locked this place up. Now I was gonna have to go back to Mrs. Porter and ask her for a way out. Or maybe this was part of her plan. Maybe she *wanted* me to find the door locked so I'd be forced to spend more time in this hellhole.

I turned around and saw someone standing at the top of the stairs.

It startled me, at first. Startled me because I didn't recognize the figure. They were dressed in the same blue overalls that the janitor wore, but their face... it was different.

Paler. A more vacant look. Glasses wonky on his nose.

"Scuse—scuse me?" I said. "The door. It's locked. I need to get outta here. Please."

I realized how pathetic I sounded. I knew I sounded frightened. And it didn't help that this janitor was standing up there all scarily, not saying a word back to me.

Just tilting his head, side to side, in a robotic manner.

I looked to my left. Another classroom. Maybe I could go in there and climb out of a window. Hell, I could use my ULTRA abilities to get through the door or the wall if I wanted to. But now the janitor was here, I'd definitely need to get out of sight before using them.

I went to walk into the classroom when I felt a presence right beside me.

When I turned, I saw the janitor raising his fist.

He swung it at me. And I didn't even have time to react with my abilities. I went crashing back into the wall. Crashing back with immense force.

I slid to the floor. My back wrecked with pain. I tasted blood in my mouth from where I'd bit my tongue.

The janitor walked towards me again, in that robotic manner.

Lifted his fist.

I swung out of the way as quickly as I could. I spun into the air, dodged his—

Even though I jumped up using my super-speed, the janitor's punch still connected with me.

Sent me hurtling through that classroom door, knocking all the chairs over in the process.

I lay back on the floor and watched as the janitor approached me. I knew right now something was wrong here. The janitor. He had strength. Serious strength. Way more strength than a normal person.

The janitor was an ULTRA?

There was another ULTRA in existence?

Even if he was, why was he...

The janitor lifted a chair and threw it at me.

I shifted it away before it hit my face. And despite the fear I felt at embracing Glacies, I was in danger right now. Self-Defense. I had to fight.

I swung out of the way of the second chair flying at me. Teleported behind the janitor, and as awkward as it felt, I cracked a punch towards his neck.

His hand swung back, his arm snapping in an impossible position. He grabbed my arm, then twisted me over to the floor.

I kicked out before I hit the ground and bounced back up towards him. I stuck both my fists together, knocked them into his chin.

But... shit!

I fell back down to the floor. My fists ached like mad.

The janitor stood over me. Stared down. My heart raced. He didn't look like he was hurt. Didn't even look like I'd scratched him.

He lifted another chair and I realized right then that I'd met my match.

That I only had one choice.

I felt the fear inside me. Felt it take over me.

The janitor swung the chair towards my face.

I lifted my hands and with all the strength I had, I fired a bolt of ice right into its face.

Something weird happened, then. Something even weirder than everything that'd already happened.

The janitor froze on the spot, not literally. But he just stopped, like he was malfunctioning.

He shook from side to side. His legs wobbled. He opened his mouth and closed it, smoke emitting from his ears.

And then he fell and hit the floor in a noisy thump.

I stood up. Waddled away from the janitor. I kept my eyes on him at all times. I didn't want to let him out of my sight.

"What... what are you?" I asked.

The janitor let out a shriek of laughter. But it was laughter that didn't sound like it belonged to this man. He looked too frail to make that laughter—as much as I knew he wasn't frail. Like it was someone else laughing through him.

"You don't understand," the janitor said, the voice sounding as if it came from somewhere deep inside him. "But you will. You will."

A buzzing noise spurted from the janitor's mouth.

Electricity crackled across his body.

And then he went still.

I stood and stared at the chaos and the destruction in the classroom and tried to figure out what'd happened.

He was right. I didn't understand. I didn't understand in the slightest.

But he was right about something else, too.

Soon, I would.

Very soon.

8

"I mean, man, did she throw a punch at you or somethin'? Never really had her down as the fighter type."

I sat in Pazza Notte opposite Damon. It was usually way out of our price range, and we didn't tend to go to posh restaurants—unless McDonalds counted. But we'd got some vouchers at school so Damon insisted we went and made ourselves look extra posh. Besides, what else was I gonna do? I didn't have Ellicia to see anymore.

The chatter around the restaurant blurred around me. I heard glasses clinking together, the laughter of men and women as they enjoyed their dates. The smell of the pizza cooking didn't make me want to eat it, as much as I loved pizza. Even the friendliness of the staff annoyed me.

I was trapped in a rut. And not just because Ellicia was moving to Arizona in three weeks.

But also because of what happened with that weird robot-y janitor yesterday afternoon.

It was Saturday now, so I hadn't really had much chance to talk about it with anyone. And I wouldn't get a chance either. When I got myself back home, I lay in bed and thought about what I was going to do, playing over events. If that janitor were found lying there, then surely the school would find a way to trace it back to me, and then my powers would be blown. I was stupid. I'd used Glacies' powers without even having my costume on. I'd risked exposing my entire identity, my entire life.

So I'd gone back there. Gone back to take the janitor away somewhere. To hide him, or something.

Weird thing happened when I got back.

The janitor was gone.

The classroom was completely tidy and in order.

The door was a bit loose on the hinges, sure. But not enough to attract any real attention.

"You even listening to me?"

I snapped out of my thoughts as well as I could. "Sorry. What were you saying?"

"That bruise under your eye. How the hell'd you get that?"

I didn't know what Damon was talking about until I caught a glimpse of my reflection on my phone screen. "Shit," I said.

"What happened?"

Damn. I must've been so caught up with everything that'd been going on that I'd forgotten to heal myself properly. "Just, um... just fell down the stairs."

"Fell down the stairs? What are you, ninety?"

"I was carrying something hot and I slipped, okay?"

Damon shrugged. Took a sip of his Coca-Cola. "I'm just sayin'. If Ellicia's the violent type, maybe you wanna report that shit."

I shook my head. "She's not the violent type. Far from it."

"Well she broke your damned heart. Far as I can tell, that's a pretty violent thing to do."

I leaned back in my chair and waited for our meal to arrive. I didn't want to be here. I wanted to be back home on my own.

But I knew deep down that I couldn't mope. I had to see my friends. If anyone could put a smile on my face, it was Damon.

Just wasn't doing the best job right now.

"I can't feel angry at her," I said. "No matter how hard I try. 'Cause it's not *her* fault."

"The bruise under your eye isn't her fault?"

"No, the move. The move isn't her fault."

"Oh," Damon said, chewing on a piece of the bread put out for an appetizer. "Yeah, well, it's like I say. These things come and go in waves."

"What does that even mean?"

Damon shrugged, his mouth stuffed with bread. "You know. We're gettin' older. You two've had your time together. Maybe it's time you found someone new."

The thought of finding someone new made me feel even sicker than the thought of that janitor ULTRA that attacked me in school. Ellicia was part of the reason I felt so much better about myself these days. She was the goal, the benchmark, and I'd reached her.

Only the benchmark had snapped, and I didn't know what the goal was anymore. My whole life was crumbling around me. A life I'd been determined to hold on to. A life I wasn't letting go—a life I was *choosing* over a life full-time as Glacies.

What was the point anymore?

What was the point in Kyle Peters if Ellicia wasn't at the end of it?

"Your mains, gents," the waiter said. He put down two enormous pizzas in front of us. They looked delicious, sure, and I saw Damon's greedy eyes widen. But the last thing I wanted to do was eat right now.

"I, er, I think I'll head to the..."

It was at that point that I saw a woman standing over by the bar. She was older than me, probably in her early twenties. She had chocolate brown hair, sparkling blue eyes, an intoxicating combination. She was looking right into my eyes as she held on to her cocktail, smiling.

I looked away, blushing. Damon had a whole slice of pizza wedged in his mouth.

"Wha-uh?" he asked, unable to speak for the food.

I swallowed a lump in my dry throat and turned around to look at the bar.

I couldn't see the woman anymore.

I stood up. Headed to the restroom. When I got inside there, I couldn't believe the bruise under my eye. It looked like I'd been in some kind of brawl, or taken a beating. Which I had, technically. Silly of me not to cover it up. Foolish of me not to—

"You want to get some cream on that," a voice said.

I turned around and saw the woman from the bar standing by the entrance to the men's room. She was tall. Taller than I'd realized when I saw her from a distance. She had something about her, as she stood there in that long black dress. Like she had a presence in the room just by standing there.

"I, um, this is the men's," I said.

She smiled. Walked towards me. "Oh, I know."

I wasn't sure how to handle this situation. I dried my hands on some paper towels, and then I stepped outside the restroom.

When I reached the door, I felt a hand on my back.

And then the woman pulled me back into the restroom.

Pulled me with serious force.

She slapped me. Slapped me hard across my face. The flirtatious, intoxicating look was gone from her face now. She looked mad. Angry.

In fact, she looked... completely different.

Fiery red hair.

Dark eyes.

Pale skin.

Shorter.

"You need to step the shit up, Glacies," she said, her voice deeper.

When she said my name, I felt my gut turn. "How—"

"There's a storm coming. And we need you there when it arrives. We need your help."

I wanted to tell this woman I didn't understand what she was saying. That I didn't have a clue what she was talking about.

But then I remembered the janitor. The robotic mannerisms. The way he'd fallen and malfunctioned like he was nothing more than a machine.

"You've seen it," the woman said, shifting back to her former self. I knew at this point that she was an ULTRA. She had to be. "I know you've seen it. And you're afraid. That's natural. So you should be."

I backed away from the woman. Her perfume was so strong that it felt like it was luring me in.

She leaned into my ear. "You need to be Glacies. You need to stop fighting. Because soon, you won't have a choice."

I wanted to ask her what she was talking about. What she needed me to do.

And then the restroom door peeked open.

The first person I saw was Damon, grinning at me like he always did when he thought he was surprising me in a good way.

But then I saw the person beside him.

I saw the look of shock on her face, as this woman held on to me, leaned in.

"Ellicia?"

She went red. Bright red. Even Damon's jaw dropped.

"That's it," Ellicia said, her jaw shaking. She turned around, started to walk away.

"Wait!"

"That's it!"

I listened to Ellicia walk away. Damon stayed there, gawping at the pair of us in the restroom.

"I'll, um," he said, pointing in Ellicia's direction.

He checked out the woman holding on to me and then he scooted off, leaving the restroom door to close.

Before the door closed properly, he looked back at me, stuck his thumbs up and winked.

The woman's eyes sparkled. She smiled at me, flirtatiously, or how I imagined flirtatiousness looked. "She's just a girl, anyway. What you need is a woman. Seeing as you're a big, strong man really."

I shook my head. "Who are you?"

"I call myself Angel," the woman said. "And you know my associates. And we know you too. Very well."

Angel. Associates who knew me well. What was this? What was any of this?

"You need to give up this life. It's only going to cause more chaos. More pain." She was speaking more reasonably now. More to the point after her display earlier. "Trust me. I've been there. All of us have."

I thought about what she was saying. About how I had to give up my normal life because something was off. Something *was* wrong; I knew that.

But I wasn't giving anything up.

I wasn't letting me and Ellicia end like this.

I pushed past Angel. "You've got the wrong guy."

"I haven't, Glacies. I haven't got the—"

"Just leave me alone, okay?"

My shout was so loud that the entire restaurant looked around as I walked through the restroom door.

Angel looked back at me through the swinging door, a sad smile on her face. "Okay," she said, her image shifting every time the door swung back and forth. "But you'll regret it. You'll regret not taking my advice when the day comes. And that day will come very soon."

I watched the door swing again, watching Angel's appearance change once more.

When the door swung a final time, Angel was gone.

9

I stormed out of Pazza Notte and chased after Ellicia.

I pushed past people as I rushed down the sidewalk. Behind, I could hear Damon calling out at me, telling me to stop being an idiot, to come back. I'd sat with him after leaving the restroom just to cool off, calm down. Get to grips with what'd just happened. I'd been confronted by another ULTRA. I mean, she *had* to be an ULTRA with the ability to change her looks with the click of a finger, right?

I knew what this meant. I wasn't alone. I'd suspected as much after the janitor attacked me, but this... this was different.

And oh. She'd asked me to join some weird secret club of hers.

But most importantly, Ellicia was leaving me. She'd spotted me and she thought something crazy was going on. That, I couldn't take.

I didn't want her to think I'd been unfaithful with... with *whoever* that woman who called herself "Angel" was.

I thought about her words. *"There's a storm coming. And we need you there when it arrives."* And I felt it. I felt it coming just as she'd said.

But I also felt my life as a seventeen-year-old falling apart. And for me, right now, that meant a whole lot more.

"Ellicia!" I called. More people looked at me like I was crazy as I rushed down Avenue of the Americas. I realized how weird I looked. Ellicia would be way, way ahead by now.

The sky was dark, the sun setting earlier and earlier as winter progressed. There was an icy chill in the air and patches of snow on the ground. Sprinkles of it fell from the sky. I knew it was only going to get snowier the further into winter we got. That was just the New York way.

"Ellicia!" I called again. I felt my cheeks heating up. Saw a group of tourists with cameras frowning at me, a few of them giggling. I realized then that I hadn't even grabbed my coat from Pazza Notte before I left. No wonder I was so damned cold. Hopefully, Damon would pick it up for me.

I reached the edge of the sidewalk. Looked up and down, all around. No sign of Ellicia. Nothing but the bustle of a Manhattan winter's night. I knew right then that I only had one choice. I had to go back to Staten Island. I had to go to her place. I knew her parents, and they were alright with me. But I saw myself as if from outside my own body—the weird boyfriend, no, *ex*-boyfriend begging his girlfriend not to leave him.

I didn't want to be that guy. I never, ever wanted to be that guy.

But right now, I was going to have to be.

I couldn't stop Ellicia leaving New York. That was just a hard fact I had to learn to swallow.

But I couldn't let her leave thinking I was an enormous asshole.

I rushed down the steps towards the subway. It was so busy down here, the smell of hot metal rich in the air. I sat and waited for the train that'd get me to the ferry. Beside me, loads of people all shouting at the tops of their voices, laughing, singing.

I felt my skin creeping. I just wanted to get out of this place. I just wanted to get the hell away.

Finally, the subway arrived. I saw the doors open up and... shit. The train was absolutely full. Absolutely jam-packed.

And it was only filling up more and more with the people from the platform.

I tried to push my way towards the door, to squeeze my way inside it. I had to get to Ellicia's place. She couldn't have got away from here long before me. Unless she'd got on the train as soon as she'd got down here. She could be on a ferry in no time.

"Sorry, man. Ain't gonna fit on here."

I looked ahead to see a chunky guy with short, dark hair and glasses holding up his hand. He was wedged right in by the train door, taking up the space of about four people.

I felt my fists hardening. "I'm sure I can—"

"No. You can't. Step away."

My stomach turned. In that split second, I wanted to grab this fatty. I wanted to throw him off the train.

"Maybe if *you* moved, another eight of us would be able to fit on there."

I saw the man's eyes narrow. Saw his face go red.

"Wow," a woman beside the guy said, glaring at me. "What an asshole."

I realized right then that I wasn't going to get my way. I wasn't getting on this train, whether I wanted to or not. And I really did want to.

The next train was in... shit. Twenty minutes. I didn't have twenty minutes. I had to get to Ellicia's *now*.

And there was only one way I was getting to Ellicia's ASAP for sure.

I left the station. Walked back up onto Ave of the Americas. I looked around for somewhere dark, somewhere secluded. Places like that were hard to find around here in Midtown.

I cut across towards Central Park. That place got busy in the day, but people avoided the darker areas at night. Rumors of crime, general paranoia, things like that. It kept people away.

Which was exactly why I had to go that way right now.

I walked into the darkened Central Park. Little spotlights lined the pathways, the roads, but the fields and the woods were jet black.

They were the kind of jet-black I needed right now.

I started to cut off the road towards the field when I became aware of footsteps to my left. I didn't look up. I didn't want to draw any attention to myself. Besides, they weren't coming towards me. The crime on Central Park thing was just a myth. A tourist scare story—

I felt something sharp press into my back. Felt someone grab my shoulder.

Then, a voice: "Your phone. Your wallet. Now."

I felt my stomach sink. "I don't have time for this shit right now."

The voice behind me, sour breath accompanying it, chuckled a little. "Well, don't you worry, boy. I got all the time in the wor—"

I swung around and cracked my fist into the guy's face. Hard.

And then I kicked the knife from his hand. Jumped over to it before he could reach it. He rested there on the ground, startled, his eyes wavering.

"You didn't see a thing here," I said.

And then I held my breath.

Focused on Ellicia, on our breakup, on the way I'd felt when she told me she was leaving New York.

I felt the tingling sensation cover my body...

Clapped my hands together.

A bang.

And then I was there.

I stood outside Ellicia's home on Staten Island. It was a nice little detached place with a picket fence, certainly in a much nicer neighborhood than mine. I saw a light was on downstairs, so I knew someone was home.

I just had to hope it was Ellicia.

Just had to hope she'd made her way back already. Getting to the park, fighting there, all of it had held me back. I hoped to God she was home already.

I swallowed a nauseating lump in my throat and walked towards her front door. As I walked up the garden path, my head spun with questions. What was I going to say to Ellicia? What would I say to her parents? What was I even doing here?

Damn. I was about to find out.

I raised my fist to knock on the white door.

Before I could knock, I heard the door lock clunk, then someone open it up.

"Oh!" Ellicia's mom, Sally, stood at the door in her white dressing gown. She was a short woman with long, dark hair, and dark skin. "Kyle. You okay? Ellicia just got back. Wasn't expecting you to be with her."

I wasn't sure what to say, how to respond, so I just nodded and smiled. "Can I, um..."

Sally nodded. "Yeah. Yeah, course you can. She's just through there. Absorbing the news, y'know. Like we all are. Go on. Go through."

The news that they were moving. The news that the pair of us weren't going to be together much longer. If Ellicia was absorbing it, I supposed that was a good thing. It meant I could still win her round with an apology.

When I walked through into Ellicia's living room, she wasn't how I expected.

She was sitting right in front of the wall-mounted sixty-inch television, which I was insanely jealous of. Her eyes were glued to the screen, the rest of the room in darkness. Her dad's eyes were also absorbed with whatever events were unfolding on there.

"Ellicia," I said, walking towards her, "I'm sor—"

"Doesn't matter anymore," Ellicia said, not moving her eyes from the television. "Haven't you seen the news?"

I couldn't believe Ellicia. Couldn't believe she'd just let what happened go, just like that. Still, she looked at the screen. So too did her dad.

And then I remembered what her mom said. About "absorbing the news".

What had she meant after all?

Had she meant something else?

"What news?" I asked.

Ellicia lifted her hand. Pointed at the television screen.

It took me a few seconds to truly take in the information on the screen. To truly comprehend what I was looking at.

When I did, for not the first time in the last year, my life changed.

Forever.

10

It took me a while to absorb the news report on Ellicia's television.

And when I did absorb it, when the news finally sunk in, I still wasn't sure I'd wrapped my head completely around it. I'm not sure anyone would be able to.

Especially not me.

The news report was of a cruise ship off the coast of Mexico. A British company, one of these Caribbean and Central American tours. A winter getaway to some place nicer.

Only it wasn't nicer. Not anymore.

That cruise ship was on fire.

At first, when I saw that report, standing closer to Ellicia's television screen now, I'd just assumed there'd been some accident. Some kind of disaster. Flames were coming from the ship. The entire mid-section of it had been snapped in two.

But it was those words rolling underneath the news story that caught me. That caught everyone.

ULTRA ATTACK DEVASTATES CRUISE VACATION.

I read those first two words over and over. *ULTRA attack.* *ULTRA attack.* It could only mean one thing. Yet another

ULTRA was back. An ULTRA I didn't know about somewhere else in the world. And, just like Nycto had, and Saint before him, they were attacking innocent people.

"They could be wrong," I muttered, not really planning on saying anything to split the silence in Ellicia's living room, but more thinking aloud.

"No," Ellicia's dad, Mike, said. He hadn't once looked away from the screen since I'd stepped into the room. I was surprised he even knew I was there. "Look."

I saw them chatting about the event in the studio, tons of panic in their voices. And then I saw them go back to that footage. Slow it down.

I didn't need to focus to see it this time.

There was someone hovering above the cruise ship, no doubt about it. Electricity sparked from their hands. A man with dark hair.

They looked at the grainy camera.

They smiled.

And then they rained electricity down on that cruise ship.

I watched the explosion. Watched the panic and chaos it caused.

And then I watched as the ULTRA disappeared out of shot, away from the cruise ship.

"They're back," Mike said. "They... they're really back."

I felt like I could throw up. I didn't know what to say or what to think, only that if there was another rogue ULTRA about, I had a duty as Glacies to stop it.

But by becoming Glacies, I was risking everything in my normal life. By become Glacies, I was...

"And we've got reports coming through of a *second* attack. A —a second attack at Disney World, Florida." The newsreader put a hand to her ear as the news broke through to her, the news that stunned the whole living room—and probably the whole world—to silence once more. "I'm hearing news that it's not the same ULTRA. I repeat. It's a different ULTRA. There's more than one ULTRA on the attack."

I wasn't sure what was said after that. Not on the television, not in this room. I saw the images, though. The grainy footage of the roller coasters destroyed. And then I saw the flames burning. Saw the shots of someone dressed in black throwing explosive balls of smoke into the theme park.

And that wasn't the last incident.

Over the next hour, two hours, that followed, there were eight more attacks around the world. Eight places where people were just having fun, going about their business, joining the two places that'd already been attacked.

Ten paths of destruction.

And most importantly, ten different ULTRAs.

I could handle one, sure. I could probably handle two. But ten?

Ten plus?

"There's a storm coming. And we need you there when it arrives."

I stood up, my legs weak and wobbly. "I need to, um, to leave."

Mike looked around for the first time. "Sure you're okay getting back? Need a ride?"

"No," I said. "I'd better, um... better check Mom and Dad are okay. You know."

Mike nodded, then returned to his television. Ellicia looked at me with concern in her eyes.

"You'll be okay, won't you?" she asked.

I swallowed a lump in my throat. Tried to smile as well as I could. If I looked as sick as I felt, I was amazed nobody had figured out I was an ULTRA already. "We'll talk. Tomorrow."

"Tomorrow," Ellicia said, nodding.

"Well shit. President's out, and he's gunnin' for action."

I was about to leave when I saw what Mike was talking about. President Marko was standing at his podium, the flags of the United States and the world behind his back. By his side, some people I didn't recognize, all suited and all remorseful. One of them stared on, deathly and grave, a look in their eyes like they weren't even human at all.

"Obviously," the president started, "we do not understand what is happening. We do not understand how this awful sequence of events might've unfolded. But we can promise that we won't sit back. Not again. After the chaos of the last two ULTRA battles, we can't just wait for a false prophet to save us again. So that's why we've been building something. Working on something in case a day like this ever arrived. I regret to say, ladies and gentlemen, that the day has arrived. I hand over my friend, Mr. Parsons, who'd like to talk you through an immediate change in global security."

The president stepped aside, and a tall man with dark hair and glasses stepped up to the podium. Something about him made me shiver. Gave me the creeps. Something about him told me I'd met him before, seen him before somewhere. Probably next to the president during another of his speeches.

He looked down at the podium, as if glancing through lines, then he looked up at the onlooking media.

"The ULTRA threat has never been graver than it is today, right now, at this moment. I never thought we'd reach this point. I hoped we wouldn't reach this point. But the truth of the matter is, the fallout from the Great Blast and the fallout from Glacies and Nycto's showdown clearly started something. They created a threat far greater than any we could've imagined."

I wasn't sure what to make of his accusation that mine and Nycto's conflict in some way created more of these ULTRAs. It didn't seem... right.

"But we've been preparing. Not just the United States, but the whole world. Our allies in NATO, our friends in the EU. Even countries with values that differ to ours. All of us have sat down and recognized the need for a security overhaul in the worst case scenario that a day like today ever unfolds. I'm both honored and disappointed to be forced to announce our latest project. The ULTRAbots."

Mr. Parsons raised his hand and pointed at the man that had been standing beside him that I noticed earlier. The one with the steely gaze, the amazingly neutral expression despite the circumstances.

The man stepped forward. He was tall, slim, and for the first time since the broadcast started, I noticed he was wearing a strange gray suit. Like a *hero* suit. On it, a silver crest, like a lightning bolt.

He stood at the podium. He stared out at the crowd, but it wasn't like he was *really* looking at them. It wasn't like he was really even there.

"We've embraced what we've learned from the creation of the ULTRAs and we've put it towards something new. Instead of the ULTRAs being able to make weapons of themselves, subject to their own moral and ethical standards, the ULTRAbots are *our* weapon. Humanity's weapon against not just ULTRAs, but everything from petty theft to terrorism. Everything. They are the second generation of security. The ULTRAs—formerly known as Heroes—were the alpha project. This is the final model."

I felt sick. I didn't know what to think about any of this, but I could see where it was going. The janitor I'd fought at the school. The robotic way it moved. The way it malfunctioned. It was an ULTRAbot. It was one of these *things*.

I swore I saw a smile on Mr. Parsons' face as he looked

down at the podium once more. Maybe it was just my imagination, but I definitely noticed something.

"I understand your concerns," he said, as the cameras flashed, as chatter picked up amongst the crowd of press. "I understand your fears. We made mistakes with the ULTRAs in the past. How will this be any different? Well, ladies and gents, this will be different because we can program the ULTRAbots. Just like a blank hard drive, we can install whatever OS we desire onto it. And right now, we've only got one thing installed on these ULTRAbots. Only one goal for them. One purpose."

He walked around the back of the ULTRAbot. Put his hand on it. It didn't even flinch.

"The ULTRAbots are programmed to hunt down every single ULTRA on the planet, whether we know their identity or not. They are programmed to capture and destroy, where possible, every single ULTRA. To keep the world safe."

I saw a sudden shift in the eyes of the ULTRAbot. I saw it come to life, like it had an idea in its mind.

And then I saw it look directly down the camera.

Look directly into my eyes like it knew I was there.

"For the ULTRAs out there," Mr. Parsons said, his hand still on the back of the ULTRAbot, "I have a message for you. The United States of America has a message for you. The whole world has a message for you. You will *not* defeat humanity!"

The press roared. People stood, applauded. Even Mike started clapping, and I swore I saw a smile on Ellicia's face.

I needed to get away.

I needed to get out of here.

"And this is just one ULTRAbot," Mr. Parsons said. "One ULTRAbot joining an army of hundreds. Thousands. An army that is growing every second; that is getting stronger every minute."

Mr. Parsons looked into the camera this time.

"You can try to run. You can try to hide. But this time, you will not succeed."

More clapping from the press. More applause. A big grin on the face of the president.

Mr. Parsons looked down the camera, right into my eyes.

"The ULTRAbots will destroy every trace of ULTRAs on this planet. Within a week."

The ULTRAbot sprung to life, shot up, right through the roof of the press room, knocking dust and rubble down with it.

I listened to the cheering, to the applause, to the joy, and I wanted to disappear.

11

I lay on my bed and stared at the ceiling as the events of earlier replayed in my mind.

It was the middle of the night. Well, early hours of the morning. That's what everyone means when they say "the middle of the night," right? I hadn't got a wink of sleep even though it had to be some time past three a.m., 'cause I'd checked my phone a short while back and it'd been 2:50. Outside, I could hear a strong breeze rattling at my window. I could feel the foundations of my house creaking. The snowstorm was strong, apparently, and it was going to hit New York for six. Flights would be delayed. Vacations in the city would be canceled. Transport was going to come to an absolute standstill.

But nobody cared because the government had just declared war on the "terrorist" ULTRAs raining chaos on the world.

Nobody cared because the ULTRAbots were going to protect them, save their lives.

Nobody cared but me. An ULTRA who was going to be hunted down by those very ULTRAbots.

I tried to close my eyes, but all I saw was that broadcast. The president's speech. Mr. Parsons and his defiant stance. The introduction of the ULTRAbots—a radically new form of security designed for one reason only: to hunt down ULTRAs.

They hadn't gone into specifics. They hadn't explained how the ULTRAbots worked, how they were able to hunt down ULTRAs. But they'd talked about programming and I knew that meant they had to have a way of detecting who was an ULTRA and who wasn't. They had to have a way of deciphering the good from the bad. And to the world, ULTRAbots were good because ULTRAbots were on the side of humanity.

ULTRAs were bad, all over again.

I wondered whether anyone had spared a thought for Glacies. If they'd remember what he—I—had done for the world. I'd taken down Nycto. I'd risked everything to protect humanity. And now the people of the world were going to allow the governments to hunt people like me down, just like they were hunting down the rest of those attackers. Because to them, I was just the same.

I remembered Angel's words. *"There's a storm coming. And we need you there when it arrives."* And now more than ever, I heard her loud and clear.

She'd spoken of fighting. Just like the Man in the Bowler Hat told me I had to kill my Kyle Peters identity if I wanted to survive, that I couldn't live two lives 'cause it was too dangerous; she wanted me to give everything up.

But I wasn't ready to give everything up. I was a seventeen-year-old with a whole life ahead of me. Sure, Ellicia had broken up with me, but I still didn't want to accept it was over.

I wanted to be able to live my two lives just like I was supposed to all along, just like I had been doing these last six months since taking down Nycto.

I got out of bed. I knew I wouldn't be able to rest. I looked out the window at my street. The snow was falling heavier than

I thought. Tomorrow, they'd have to plow the streets, and people would have to shovel snow off their cars. I thought about Dad and the work on the car I'd done with him. The lessons we were supposed to be going on. If I gave up on Kyle Peters and fought back against the ULTRAbots, I'd give up on that. If I gave up on Kyle Peters, I'd be giving up on Damon. On Ellicia. On college. On everything.

If I gave up on Kyle Peters, I gave up on life.

Right now, I wasn't ready to give up on life.

I walked back over to my bed. I didn't lie down on it, just sat on the edge of it, put my face into my cold hands.

I wished there was an easier way to make this decision. But no doubt the ULTRAbots would be targeting the ULTRAs who'd launched those devastating attacks first. I wondered who those ULTRAs even were. Where they'd come from. Why they were attacking innocent people. It all seemed so off. All seemed so strange.

And for some reason, I couldn't get Mr. Parsons' smirk when he looked back down at the podium out of my mind.

But the fact was, the ULTRAbots would target the attackers first. People wanted retribution. They wanted revenge. That would be the way they started.

And for all the fist-pumping and bravado, I wondered if those ULTRAbots could really *trace* ULTRAs. That was surely just something the government was saying to make people feel safer. Their targets would be the attackers. The real enemies. Everyone else was safe, however many "everyone else" was.

I thought about Angel and wondered where she stood on this. What she meant. How she knew the storm was coming.

But I knew there wasn't a thing I could do about it.

I lay back on my bed. Stared up at the ceiling. Listened to the crackling of the heating, the whirr of the wind.

I had to leave the government, the ULTRAbots, to do their job.

There was nothing I could do to fight. There were too many people I cared about. Too many people in this life I wasn't giving up on. Not for anything.

And the world Angel offered... well, that world was scary. That was a world I wasn't ready for. It was a door to someplace dark and unknown that I wasn't sure I wanted to even peek inside because just peeking inside would rob me of who I really was.

Kyle Peters.

I closed my eyes. Swallowed a lump in my throat.

I wasn't giving myself up.

I wasn't giving the life I'd been living up.

I was just going to keep a low profile for as long as I had to, just like I had been doing for six months.

I was going to fight for both my lives. I was going to do whatever I had to.

As sleep finally approached, I dreamed of screams, of explosions, of thrashing and murmuring as someone held my little body underwater.

12

Bowler stood on the rooftop of his Chelsea apartment and wished today's news had turned out... different. Very different.

The night was black, but it was lit up with the fall of snow. It was cold and frosty, and Bowler knew he must be mad to be up here, all on his own, foregoing sleep just after he'd learned of the greatest threat to his existence since... well, since Saint.

After all, he *was* Orion.

He *was* the one who'd caused the Great Blast.

He looked down at all the buildings. Imagined the people lying in their beds, sleeping soundly now they knew the ULTRAbots were on their way to take down every ULTRA in existence. The claims had been strong, and unlike anything he'd expected. Sure, he'd often wondered how long it'd be before the government attempted to attack the ULTRAs that they knew were out there—ULTRAs like him.

But the way everything had played out. The ten attacks in a row, all over the world, by ULTRAs, some of whom looked familiar, but most of which seemed... unfamiliar.

It was strange, to say the least.

"Question: why always the damned rooftop? Why not a nice warm cafe with a cup of coffee? And why five a.m.?"

Bowler turned around and saw Angel standing by his side. He hadn't heard her come up here. But that was part of what she was so good at. Not only was she extremely sneaky and quiet, but she could shift her form, too. You could see someone on the street, and it could be Angel. You could see your friend; it could be Angel. He hadn't met anyone quite as strong, quite as powerful a shapeshifter, since Saint.

"Don't you read the papers?" Bowler asked.

Angel wiped some snow from her shoulders. She was wearing a long, black overcoat. Her legs were bare around her ankles. She was wearing heels without socks. No wonder she was cold. "Does anyone read the papers nowadays? No. No, but I saw the news alright. Saw it clear. The ULTRAs, the government. How d'you think it's going down?"

Bowler looked back out over the city. The lights of the distant Midtown looked so pretty at this hour. So relaxing. Sometimes he wished he could throw himself into those lights and let all his responsibilities go. "Roadrunner claims it's a breakout. Over at Area 64."

Angel nodded. "That'd figure. Always wondered about that place, especially after what Kal said when he actually did manage to get out. Could never get near it after that. Fried if we went within inches of it."

Bowler thought back to that day four years ago. One of their friends, Kal, had heard talk of a prison for ULTRAs over in the Mojave Desert. It added up because a lot of ULTRAs—all of whom were laying low after the showdown between Saint and Orion—were going missing out of the blue. Only Kal got caught, and he got out claiming he'd seen all sorts of horrors, more imprisoned ULTRAs than anyone could imagine.

Kal also said he heard talks that the government was

working on things, too. Experimenting on live ULTRAs to create the perfect ULTRA. An ULTRA that bent totally to humanity's will.

The final product.

Kal went completely insane soon after.

"I'm thinking some kinda setup," Angel said, rubbing her arms. Her hair looked thicker and darker than it did when Bowler last looked at her. Adapting to the climate. "I'm thinking the government had those ULTRAs trapped in Area 64 just so that they could find an excuse to release 'em one day. Release the ULTRAs, cause a bitta mayhem, then bingo—there's the excuse for launching the ULTRAbots. 'Saving the world.' Really, all it is is an excuse for increased security. For suffocating democracy and freedom even more. All in the name of freedom. All in the name of fear."

Bowler considered Angel's theory. It was a good one, and a perfectly valid one at that. It was a theory he'd thought about and considered himself a few times.

"Well?" Angel said. "Anything? Or am I gonna have to beg you for an answer?"

"Kyle Peters," Bowler said, changing the subject. "Glacies. How did he react to your visit?"

Angel rolled her eyes and brushed her hair out of her face. It thinned with a twitch, turned a lighter shade. "Oh, he was a waste of space. Too worried about some girl or other to give a damn about what I had to say."

Bowler felt a speck of anger twinge inside. "I told you to be straight with him. To be direct."

"Have you ever tried being direct with a teenage boy in the bathroom? A teenage boy who's desperate to get out? No. I didn't think so. If you have, well. That's the kinda stunt that gets men in black coats and bowler hats arrested."

Bowler turned away. He felt annoyed at Kyle, especially

after the single conversation they'd had in the past. He'd kept a close eye on Kyle in the last six months. After he had defeated Nycto, he'd watched him living an ordinary life as a teenager. He'd watched him go on dates, kiss Ellicia. He'd almost felt happy for the boy.

How couldn't he feel happy for the boy? Kyle was his son.

But there was something else he felt when he saw Kyle, too. Annoyance. Irritation. Because Kyle was spending some of his time as Glacies. He was averting crime situations. He was thwarting attacks. He was keeping a low profile, sure, but not low enough. And Bowler knew Kyle thought he was invincible and invisible if he kept out of the public eye. He thought he could go on living a double life.

But he was wrong.

He was so, so wrong.

And if the rise of the ULTRAbots didn't make him realize that, he wasn't sure what would.

"Anyway," Angel said. "I'm through with that jackass. He's all yours. Now let's talk ULTRAbots. Let's talk strategy. And strategy does not include standing on an apartment roof like some cliche movie superhero and 'musing' as we stare into the night."

Contrary to Angel's wishes, Bowler didn't speak for a short while. Not because he was superficially "musing," but because things like this genuinely did take him time to work out, to figure out. He'd always liked to think things through, deeply. Deep thought was the best way to avert a crisis, to avoid chaos.

And as much as he knew he should be thinking about the ULTRAbots right now, it was Kyle Peters in his mind.

Because he needed Kyle Peters. Everyone needed Kyle Peters. Kyle was strong. Stronger than him, stronger than everyone.

Because he'd created him.

His mind wandered to the water. To the fight back of that baby. To the arguing, to being told he shouldn't do this 'cause it was morally wrong, ethically wrong.

But he'd known right then when he'd held Kyle down that he was doing the right thing.

He couldn't be Orion anymore. Not as strong as he was. He'd had to change his identity. He'd become too accustomed to that sheer level of power, and he needed to balance it out, so he didn't accidentally cause chaos again, just like he had with the Great Blast.

He knew that power would awaken in young, innocent Kyle Peters one day, just as it had with him all those years back.

He just wished he'd had more time to guide Kyle on his journey from ULTRA to true Hero.

"So anyway, genius. What you reckon? Mind-washed ULTRAs released from jail and told to attack the public? Wouldn't be the first time."

"I'm not sure," Bowler said.

Angel narrowed her eyes. "You ain't sure? I didn't stay awake till five a.m. for you not to be sure."

"The ULTRAs I saw. The ones committing the attacks. I didn't recognize any of them. Just the first one. An ULTRA specializing in electricity who I know as Bolt. I believe he was imprisoned in Area 64 many years ago."

Angel paused. "Bolt. Original. Anyway. Your point is?"

"It just seems... weird, that's all. I mean, they didn't have the same demeanor as the ULTRAbots. And several of them I didn't recognize as escapees from Area 64; ULTRAs that went missing around the time."

"But you can't pretend to know every ULTRA in existence, man. Maybe they were ones Area 64 picked up from the other side of the world, y'know?"

Bowler thought about the looks on those ULTRAs' faces as they'd caused chaos all over the world. "Maybe," he said.

He didn't tell Angel what his major fear was. The younger looking ULTRAs. He didn't tell her because he didn't totally know what it meant yet.

He had a fear. A feeling.

But he didn't act on feelings.

He acted on logic.

"I just can't believe that brat's gonna let the world burn while we sit around figuring out what the hell to do."

Hearing his son described as a brat stung, but Angel had a point. Glacies was powerful. More powerful than anyone. And he was the only one capable of leading the fight against the ULTRAbots. Not just physically, but mentally, too. There was a reason Bowler couldn't use his full powers. There was a reason he couldn't fight as he used to as Orion.

He was afraid of causing any more human casualties after the Great Blast.

"Glacies will realize, in time."

"How much time?"

The images of the attacks played around Bowler's mind. The celebratory fist-pumps of the government, of the press. The way the first ULTRAbot stormed out of the ceiling as its hunt began. He wondered what the news would be when he woke tomorrow. How many ULTRAs he'd lose. How long until it was Angel, himself.

Kyle.

"Not long," Bowler said.

He turned around. Walked away from the apartment.

He really, truly believed that Glacies would realize the importance of his cooperation very soon.

He just hoped he was ready for what followed.

[13]

I didn't really want to go out into Manhattan with Damon and Avi, but I figured if I were going to carry on living my life as Kyle Peters while the ULTRAbots waged war on the ULTRAs, then I'd better stick to my damned word.

The snow was thick and crunchy underfoot. It wasn't snowing anymore, the reports of a major storm on the way strongly overstated, and the sky was blue and clear. What tourists called a perfect New York Winter's Day, just like the shots on the postcards, the promotional photos. There were a lot of people walking around the Times Square area. A woman pushing a pram. Three men dressed in suits. Two kids turning around, looking at me. It felt like everyone was watching me. Like everyone knew who I was.

I took a deep breath, tension in my body at an all time high. The lack of sleep didn't help.

Nobody was watching me. I was just being stupid. Paranoid. If I kept a low profile, I'd be fine.

"You okay, dude?"

Avi's voice was muffled. It made me jump, spin around to look at him. Damon was by his side, wrapped up in a scarf and a thick winter parka. He looked just as weirded out by me as Avi.

"Nah. He's definitely not okay," Damon said.

"What's up, bro? Bit cold for ya?"

I searched my mind for the best, most believable excuse. "It's just... it's just Ellicia. Can't stop thinking about Ellicia leaving."

Avi and Damon looked at one another and sighed. I figured by that look that I had them suitably fooled. "Man, you gotta get her outta your head," Avi said. "That dating book I told you about. The one with a 4.6 stars on Goodreads. Well, it has a 4.4 stars now, but 4.4 stars is still good. Not quite elite level, few one stars dragged that shit down, but still—"

"What're you getting at?" I asked.

"I'm just sayin'," Avi said, as we walked along through the snow, the constant noise and chatter of Times Square growing. We were out shopping for Christmas gifts. Avi wanted some M&Ms for his sister, and no matter how much I told him Amazon Prime was the answer, he still insisted on an actual trip to the M&M store. "Not being harsh, but you gotta let her go. Have a read of that book. It'll do you good."

"Right. Just like it's doing you good?"

Avi half-smiled. "Hey. I've had seven conversations with girls since I read that book. Charmed 'em like mad."

"Avi," I said, trying to hold in my frustration. I was so pissed with his insistence that a book was the answer to my problems that suddenly I *was* more upset about the Ellicia thing than the fact a band of super-frigging-powered ULTRAbots was out to get me. "Six of those girls you only ever chatted to online."

"And the seventh one? I met her. She was super-hot."

"You met her because you had Ryan Reynolds as your profile picture and she was so dumb to believe it was actually you."

Avi shrugged. "Truth stands, man. Truth stands."

The hardest part of all? I couldn't argue. I actually couldn't argue.

I kept on walking alongside them, eager not to get so caught up in conversation that I got sidetracked. I had to be alert, on guard. If the ULTRAbots were hunting ULTRAs, then they could be onto me right now. This wasn't right. It wasn't the life I'd chosen to live. I chose the life as Kyle Peters because I wanted to be free of all that ULTRA nonsense. But I couldn't walk five steps without looking over my shoulder.

"Holy... Is that what I think it is?"

I heard the amazement in Damon's voice. I'd heard that amazement recently when he'd spoken about something with awe. Something that made my skin crawl.

When I looked where Damon was pointing, right in the middle of Times Square, I seized up completely.

Hovering above the middle of Times Square was a woman. She was dressed in a loose brown cloak, with blue jeans underneath. Her hair was short, cropped close to her head.

She stared into the distance like she was asleep. Like she was hypnotized.

Like she was just waiting for something to trigger her sensors.

A silver crest, like a lightning bolt, was embossed on her cloak.

"It's an ULTRAbot," Damon said. He let out a little laugh of amazement, then looked at Avi and me. "Guys, it's an ULTRAbot! Right here in the city!"

I didn't want to go any further. I didn't want to step any closer to that thing. I knew it was dangerous. I didn't know how they worked exactly, how they traced ULTRAs. But I remembered what that man called Mr. Parsons said on the news.

"The ULTRAbots will destroy every trace of ULTRAs on this planet. Within a week."

That was the kind of promise not to be made lightly.

"Come on, guys. We gotta go see this. This is, like, a once in a lifetime thing."

"I'm—I'm not sure," I said.

Damon and Avi stopped. Turned around to look at me. "What?"

I couldn't take my eyes off the ULTRAbot, and neither could anyone else walking by it. My mouth was dry. I just wanted to be back home. I just wanted to be away from here.

"I hear they're reaction-less, bro," Avi said. "Say anythin' to 'em and they don't do a thing back. That's the kinda shit we need to test out."

"I'm not sure about this."

"Come on, wimp," Damon said, punching my arm. "Thought you'd toughened up lately?"

"My sister," I said. It was the only thing I could think of saying. The only excuse I could come up with to get out of this situation. "Cassie. It just... It brings it back. Brings it all back. I'm sorry."

Damon sighed. But he didn't demand I joined him this time, so I took that as something—a sign that his view was softening, perhaps. "It can't harm you, dude. It can't harm any of us."

If only he knew the truth.

"Come on, Kyle," Avi said. "I mean, it's up to you, sure. But we're here. We got you. Two big bros've got you."

I was about to shake my head and say no again when I saw something that sent a shiver right through my body.

The ULTRAbot wasn't staring into space anymore.

It was looking right into my eyes.

My heart pounded. The sounds all around me went fuzzy,

out of focus. I saw Damon and Avi moving in the direction of the ULTRAbot, jogging away from me, leaving me alone.

Everything was in slow motion. Me looking at the ULTRAbot. The ULTRAbot looking back at me.

The ULTRAbot knew who I was. It knew I was an ULTRA.

And it was going to kill me if I didn't hide.

I turned away from the ULTRAbot and ran down the nearest side street. I didn't look back to see if it was looking. I couldn't afford to.

I just disappeared down the side street, shaking like a leaf.

Then I pressed my back up against the wall.

Held my breath.

Teleported right across the street.

I kept on holding my breath when I appeared at the other side of the street. Kept my camouflage activated. And in the corner of my eye, I saw the ULTRAbot emerge at the other side street where I'd stood just moments ago. I saw it look around. Look all around, like a child searching for a lost toy, or a bird of prey hunting a mouse.

I held my breath, sweat dripping down my head. Felt my teeth chattering against one another.

I could do this. I was okay. I could...

The ULTRAbot disappeared from the side street.

Floated back to the middle of Times Square and resumed its watch over the people.

I let my breath out. Along with it, a sob. I planted my hands on my knees. My stomach ached, and I wanted to throw up.

They knew. They knew who I was just by looking at me. The honing thing was true. I didn't have to be even using any Glacies powers, they just... they just knew.

I had to get home. I saw that now. I had to get home and I had to hide. No, maybe not even home. Maybe somewhere at the other side of the world. But then that'd only worry my friends. That'd only increase suspicion. And if my parents reported me missing to the police and the police reported it to the government it'd all lead back to—

"Chin up, loser."

The voice came from opposite me.

Directly opposite me.

When I looked up, I saw a man.

He was in his twenties. Good-looking, if I was into that kinda thing, which I wasn't. Long, dark hair swept back over his head. Charming, sparkling smile.

He was wearing a tight blue suit.

"Ready to listen yet?" the guy said.

It was only when I saw his hands that I realized what he was.

Electricity sparked from the tips of his fingers.

14

When I saw the electricity sparking from the guy's hands, I did the only thing I could.

I held my breath.

Pulled back my fist.

Rammed it towards this guy. Hard.

But before it could reach him, before it could crack him in the jaw, I felt my hand slowing down. I could feel the electricity tingling across my knuckles, burning at my skin.

"Wait!" the guy said. "Hold it right there."

"Get away from—"

He pushed me back against the wall down the side street, which I hit with a thud. "It's cool. I'm not one of them. I'm with Bowler, man. I'm with Bowler."

I tried to work out what this guy was saying. Bowler? Who the hell was Bowler? On the street, I could hear the chatter of amazement at the ULTRAbot hovering over Times Square, not all that far away from my current position. The thought of how close it'd come to finding me after looking me right in the eyes made me taste sick in my mouth.

"You need to chill," the guy said. "Look. My name's Spark. Well, not really, but you know. We all have names—"

"Leave me alone," I said.

"Glacies, you can't walk away. You see why you can't walk away, right? Surely you see now why you can't just turn your back on us. On your people."

I wanted to walk away. I wanted to get out of this side street and far, far away from Times Square. Far away from *everywhere*. Here was another person with ULTRA abilities, using them in public, which was dangerous in itself.

Not only that, but he knew who I was. He knew I was Glacies without me having any of my gear on.

How the hell?

Was I really so bad at disguising myself?

"You need to make a call, right now," Spark said. He looked around as a couple of people walked by. Pushed me behind a dumpster so I was out of view. "You need to make a call over what you do. But even when you make that call, we aren't gonna stop knocking. 'Cause you're important to us. You've no idea how much we need you right now."

For the first time, I actually felt some sympathy for Spark. He was just after my help. He was just an ULTRA terrified of his fate, just like me.

"Make the right call, man," Spark said. "Make the right damn call. Don't screw this up."

I swallowed a lump in my throat.

Closed my eyes.

Embraced the terror inside me.

"I'm sorry."

I shot up into the air. I wasn't strong enough and didn't have enough time for teleportation right now. I had to fly away. I had to disappear somewhere. I had to...

As I flew, I felt something pulling me back. Something clinging onto me, like a weight around my ankles.

And I looked down and saw electricity sparking up into the sky. Electricity that was coming from Spark's hands.

As if in slow motion, I saw Times Square all around me. I saw the ULTRAbot, facing the opposite direction.

I tried to fly away. Tried to shake free of the electricity.

The ULTRAbot started to turn.

I tried again. But no use. I was bound by the electricity. Spark had me.

So I did the only thing I could right now.

I dropped back down to earth. Landed right beside Spark, hurting my ass in the process.

"Good job," Spark said, rubbing his hands together. "The old electricity ain't failed me yet—"

"What the hell do you want?" I shouted.

Spark smiled. "What do *I* want? I told you what I want. Bowler. The dude in the bowler hat. I want to get you to him. 'Cause he wants to see you. To talk to you. But believe me, kid. The more of us meet you, the more of us doubt you meeting him's that good an idea at all. Really not livin' up to your Glacies reputation right now, I'll tell you that much."

The dude in the bowler hat.

The Man in the Bowler Hat.

Could it be? Could he really be looking for me? Searching me out?

I remembered the Man in the Bowler Hat's—Bowler's —words.

You need to let Kyle die.

I still didn't want to believe that. I still didn't want to give up my normal life. But he'd told me something else too. He'd made me realize that if I believed in myself, I could be stronger than I ever imagined. He was right about that.

What if he was right about that other thing?

"See, I was hoping to spare the pep talk. But the way you're behaving, I reckon I'm gonna just have to go for it. We need you, man. Your *kind* needs you. The government is hunting us. And you're a tough cookie, whether you wanna admit it or not."

"I'm not your *kind*," I said.

Spark narrowed his eyes. "You what?"

"I said I'm not your kind. I'm... I'm just a kid. I just want to live my life."

Spark stuck his bottom lip out, almost mockingly. "Aw, diddums. Is the little boy not ready for the real world yet?"

"Shut up."

"Well I'll tell you something, 'Glacies'. We were all little kids like you at some stage. All little kids coming to terms with who we are. With what we can do. And as much as you wanna go on living your nice, cushy little double life, it doesn't always work out that way. It's like growing up. Someday, you can't keep sponging off your parents. You gotta move out. You gotta get a job. 'Cause it's what we do to survive. We have to make tough calls. We can't live two lives. So you gotta make that call, right now. You join us, and you help us. Or you walk away, and you kill both your lives. Your call."

I heard Spark. I heard him loud and clear. I wanted to help. I wanted to step up. I wanted to *be* as strong as I knew I could.

"I just... I'm just not ready," I said.

Spark spat an unimpressed laugh out. He shook his head, looked at me like I was dirt. "You're choosing a side, kid. Choosing a damned side, whether you know it yet or not."

Spark walked away. Walked away down the alleyway. And as he walked, I thought about calling him back. About telling him I wanted to meet Bowler. Talk with him. There was something about Bowler that made me feel... secure. Even though he terrified me, even though I had no idea who he was, I felt like I needed his judgment right now.

Besides, maybe Spark was right. Maybe I did need to step up. If I didn't, then I wouldn't just lose my freedom as Glacies—I'd lose my life as Kyle, too.

I started to see a path in front of me. A clearer path. I realized I needed to make a decision. The right decision. For myself. For my real, real self.

I went to open my mouth to shout Spark back.

But when Spark reached the opening to the sidewalk, I saw three figures swoop down from above.

Surround him.

All of them were hovering. All of them had that dead-eyed look.

All of them were ULTRAbots.

15

I watched the three ULTRAbots surround Spark and I genuinely didn't know what to do.

Specks of snow fell from the clear skies above. The sounds of Times Square, the smells from hot dog stalls, all of them blended into the background, all of them faded away.

Three ULTRAbots were heading towards Spark.

Flying at him.

They were going to finish him.

Part of me wanted to just disappear and get back home. To give up Glacies completely. It wasn't a safe world to be an ULTRA. I knew that now more than ever. I'd seen it firsthand.

But I couldn't shake off Spark's words.

I had to choose a side. If I chose the side of Kyle Peters, I'd lose anyway.

No. I had to do something here. I had to help Spark.

I focused my attention on the first ULTRAbot, a man with dark hair a little too neatly parted to be believable.

And I put all my energy into stopping it colliding with Spark. Holding him right there, inches from Spark.

"Quick!" I shouted.

Spark looked around. He ran towards me. Behind him, the second ULTRAbot—the woman I'd seen hovering over Times Square—inched closer.

I used my mind to throw the ULTRAbot I'd frozen into the second ULTRAbot, sent it flying out of the side street, into Times Square.

Spark kept on running. There was still another ULTRAbot chasing him. I knew if I weren't quick, it'd get him. Sure, he was strong, but he needed a hand right now.

I bit my lip so hard that I tasted the metallic tang of blood.

I tried to stop that third and final ULTRAbot getting closer and closer to Spark, so close to snapping at his ankles.

I could do this. I could stop it. I could—

The ULTRAbot slammed into Spark's back.

Sent him flying across the side street, right in my direction.

I watched the ULTRAbot lift its hand. But Spark spun around, sent a shot of electricity right into the ULTRAbot's face. It made it twitch and shake for a few seconds, like a malfunctioning machine.

But then it just returned to what it was doing before.

Lifting its fist.

Swinging at Spark.

I saw Spark hold it off once more. And, standing there, I knew I couldn't just watch. On Times Square, I could see dust kicking up where the other two ULTRAbots were emerging. One of them, I could take. Three of them at once? Not possible. I wasn't strong enough right now.

I lurched forward. I had to help Spark.

But then I became aware of what I looked like. I wasn't in my Glacies gear. I was just Kyle Peters, and if I did anything too crazy right now, the whole world would know I was an ULTRA, and I'd be top of everyone's hit list.

The ULTRAbot swung a fist at Spark's face.

Spark's head smacked against the ground.

I cringed at the sound of the crack. I couldn't just stand here. I couldn't just wait and watch this happen.

I had to act.

"Hey!" I shouted.

The ULTRAbot looked up. Its fist was still hovering over Spark's face, getting ready to deliver one final blow.

"Catch this," I said.

I slammed my fists together.

Flew in the direction of the ULTRAbot.

Before we could make contact, I crashed into Spark's body and teleported the pair of us back to my street with the last of the strength I had.

I stood by the side of my home. Spark leaned against the wall of my house, gasping for air. He had a nasty cut on his head, a bruise under his eye. Clearly didn't share my ability for healing.

"Wait there," I said, walking towards my house, my legs like jelly and the rest of my body not much better. "If I'm gonna help you, I need to look like Glacies."

Spark nodded. He clutched his stomach, leaned back against the wall. The sky had gone gloomy and cloudy over Staten Island, hiding that bright sun that had shone down earlier. The flakes of snow fell thicker, heavier.

I disappeared into my bedroom. And then I opened up the drawers where I stored my Glacies gear. As I unlocked the final lock, I saw my hands were shaking.

I looked up. Looked at myself in the mirror. And looking back at me, I saw Kyle Peters. Terrified Kyle Peters. Not Glacies.

I saw the seventeen-year-old guy who wanted to live his normal life.

I saw the seventeen-year-old unpopular kid who, more than anything, just wanted to get by.

But no. I couldn't be that kid. I had to be stronger than that kid. I had to protect my people.

I threw on my Glacies gear. The black costume. The dark mask. And when I'd geared up in it, I looked back in the mirror.

Every time I saw myself as Glacies, I felt stronger right away. More powerful. Because I was powerful—Spark had told me as much, as had Bowler back when we'd mysteriously met.

I just had to embrace that power. I just had to believe that—

"Help!"

The scream was deafening. Ear-piercing.

And it came from just outside my house.

I walked over to my bedroom window, my feet as heavy as lead. I didn't want to look outside. I didn't want to see what I feared—the very worst.

But I had to look. I had to see. I couldn't just walk away.

When I reached the window, what I saw was worse than I possibly imagined.

Two ULTRAbots were standing in my street. Two I'd seen back at Times Square, not including the female one I'd first seen. They must've followed us, somehow. Traced my teleportation. Shit. Shitting shit.

One of the ULTRAbots had Spark in its arms. He was struggling, trying to fire electricity at his captors. But the more that ULTRAbot held on, the weaker I saw Spark getting. The more terrified I saw his face turning.

I wanted to go down and help him. To stop them taking him away.

But then I saw the people in their houses. The people in their gardens. Standing there, applauding the ULTRAbots.

And I saw right then that I was the villain. To them, I was the enemy.

I wasn't the one who kept them safe. Not in their minds. I was everything wrong with the world. I was the thing that needed eliminating.

I watched the ULTRAbots walk away with Spark in their arms. He was bruised, his face was covered in scratches, and his outfit was burned on the chest.

He was unconscious.

I was about to step away from the window, go to the bathroom to throw up when I saw someone standing right outside my house.

She was wearing a brown cloak.

Blue jeans.

She was looking right through my bedroom window and into my eyes with that dead-eyed stare.

She wasn't a she at all.

It was the ULTRAbot from Times Square.

And it was walking towards my front door.

16

I backed away from my window and wondered what the hell I was going to do.

The ULTRAbot outside had looked at me, right in the eye. It'd seen me. And then it'd started walking towards my door. Soon, it'd be inside my home. It'd come face to face with my parents. It'd—

I heard three heavy bangs against the front door.

My heart raced. My head spun. As I stood there in my Glacies outfit, I'd never felt more defenseless as him. They were coming for me. The ULTRAbots were coming for me. I had to do something. Fast.

"Oh, sure," I heard Mom say. "Are you one of his teachers?"

I didn't hear the ULTRAbot respond. But I heard its heavy footsteps walking down my hallway, walking towards the bottom of the stairs.

I held my breath for a few seconds. Focused on teleporting away from here, on flying out...

But then I saw a flash.

A flash in my mind that froze me to the spot.

I wasn't sure how to explain it, but a vivid image erupted

in my imagination. An image of the ULTRAbot standing behind both Mom and Dad, demanding I come back. If I didn't come back, turn myself in, Mom and Dad would both die.

I saw the tears rolling down Mom's face.

I imagined Dad begging me, urging me not to go away.

And then I snapped out of the moment and heard the creaky floorboards right outside my door.

I stood still. Completely still in my bedroom. Outside, the street was silent. The only noise was my breathing and my thumping heart.

I knew I couldn't leave this place. Not after that dizzying image that flashed in my mind, gave me a headache. If I left this place, I was turning my back on Mom and Dad, leaving them for dead. I couldn't allow that to happen.

I saw myself standing there in the mirror. Saw my reflection. And, feeling so afraid, I felt stupid. Stupid for being so afraid as Glacies. But also stupid for bringing Spark back here in the first place. I'd acted, tried to help, just like he told me I had to. And what had that done for me? It'd got Spark taken away, captured by ULTRAbots.

And it'd got me hiding in my room from that same ULTRAbot I saw hovering over Times Square.

But I had to do something. I knew that. I had to move, even if the very thought of doing so was painful. I had to brace myself for that ULTRAbot entering my room, and then I had to do something about it. It was too late for running away. I had to deal with it, head on.

So I did the only thing a weak kid did when something scary lurked outside their bedroom door.

I took a few steps back and hid inside my wardrobe.

I held my breath in there. Tried to slow down the racing of my heart. It was so loud and heavy that I swore if the

ULTRAbot listened closely enough, it'd hear my heart loud and clear.

I crouched in the darkness. Bit my lip. Felt the fear inside bubbling to the surface.

The ULTRAbot's footsteps stopped, right outside my bedroom door. There was no sound.

And then I heard a handle lowering.

The door swung open, creaking on its hinges.

I made myself smaller in the wardrobe. Curled up into a ball. I didn't want to use any of my powers for fear of attracting the ULTRAbot in some way. I had to play this right. I had to go about this the right way. The only way.

I saw the shadow creep across my floor. Downstairs, I noticed Mom and Dad were silent. I hoped they were okay, wherever they were, whatever they were doing. I pictured them on their knees, just like I'd seen them in that vision, tears and fear on their faces.

I pictured them begging for their lives.

I pictured them...

No. No, they were okay. They were going to be okay. I had this. I *had* to have this.

I watched the ULTRAbot walk slowly around my room. It moved in an unrealistic manner, its footing not quite even. My pulse still raced in my skull as I held my breath, watched the ULTRAbot go over to the window and stand in the exact spot I'd been in when I looked out at it.

It stopped right there. Looked out of the window for a few seconds.

And then it turned around and looked right at the wardrobe.

I closed my eyes. I closed them because again like anyone terrified, I didn't want to see what was looking at me. I felt like if I couldn't see what was coming my way, then maybe the ULTRAbot wouldn't see me as clearly either.

But I heard the footsteps getting heavier as the ULTRAbot approached.

I heard the floorboards creaking as it stomped across them, step by step by step.

I held my breath and felt a warm tear roll down my cheek as I thought of Ellicia. As I thought of when I'd first mustered up the courage to talk to her at the soccer game. At everything we'd been through since. And now she was leaving. Now she was moving home. Now she was going away.

I felt the tingling sensation in my body change to something stronger. Something much more powerful.

I opened my eyes.

The ULTRAbot opened the wardrobe door.

"Hey, idiot."

I saw the ULTRAbot look through the wardrobe door at where it expected me to be.

But I wasn't there.

I'd shifted outside the wardrobe and right behind the ULTRAbot.

"See how you like being stuck in a box."

The ULTRAbot lifted its hand but I flew into it with full force. I grabbed it, and I felt electricity take over my body as I dragged it through space and time, as I teleported us both far away.

When I finally appeared at the other side of whatever wormhole I'd transported us through, I realized it was still snowy. It was cold. Only it was a hell of a lot snowier and colder than it was where I used to be.

I looked around. I was on the ground, on my knees. My hands stung. In front of me, I saw deep, thick snow. Flakes flew down with painful speed and intensity. If I spent any longer here, wherever here was, I knew I'd freeze.

I stood up, battling every instinct in my body telling me to teleport back home. I saw my wardrobe in the snow ahead of me. It was face down. Underneath, I saw a twisted, broken mechanical arm. The wardrobe was shaking underneath, like something was trying to get out.

I licked my dried lips, my face icy cold. I steadied my ground. Used my usual methods to build up as much energy in my body as possible.

And then I fired a bolt of ice right at the wardrobe.

The wardrobe smashed open before the ice made contact. The ULTRAbot flew towards me.

I fell back. But I kept on firing the ice at it. I kept on pushing and pushing, making sure I took this monster down.

The ice coated the ULTRAbot. Covered its entire body.

I saw its arms getting stiff. I saw its face going gray.

And then I dove out of the way as it landed right where I'd been lying.

It smashed. Smashed and shattered limb by limb, like an expensive piece of pottery.

I stood and looked at the smashed remains of the ULTRA-bot. I gasped, catching my breath in this harsh, awful wasteland. And as I stood there, I knew right then that I hadn't really achieved anything. This wasn't going to get any easier. It was only going to get harder.

This was just the beginning.

I looked into the frozen stare of the ULTRAbot, and I shot myself back home.

Explaining the wardrobe situation to my parents wasn't going to be easy.

As I DISAPPEARED, I didn't notice the ULTRAbot's eye twitch.

17

I walked through the school grounds and couldn't feel relaxed about anything.

The snow had stopped, but the cold had attacked stronger than at any point so far this winter. There was a bitterness to it as I breathed in, the kind of cold that stung your nostrils and your lungs. I had that groggy feeling at the back of my throat, too. The kind of feeling that came with not much sleep. Which didn't surprise me. I hadn't had much sleep at all these last few days.

"You sure you're okay, dude?" Damon asked. He frowned at me, much in the way he'd frowned at me a lot lately. "Swear you look more like a ghost every time I see you."

"It's just this bug," I said, fully aware that I was probably the most terrible liar in the world. I was training, though. Practicing, and trying to get better. I might've been good at being an ULTRA, but lying was still a trait I hadn't honed.

"Yeah. This mystery bug you keep goin' on about that nobody else has."

"It's winter," I said. "Bugs are what happen."

"Right," Damon said, sounding unconvinced. "The world's

falling apart, Ellicia's left you, and it's a bug that finally floors you."

I was partly pleased that Damon still thought it was the Ellicia thing that was getting to me. Of course it was. But I had way bigger problems to worry about right now. Spark. The ULTRA I'd watched get taken away by the ULTRAbots, right outside my house. I couldn't escape the guilt I felt for what happened to him. I couldn't shake the feeling that I could've done something more if I'd really tried.

"You see the news from Paris last night?" Damon asked, as we made our way up the stairs towards Geography.

I looked over my shoulder. I'd become increasingly panicky when I was in school–well, when I was anywhere–especially after the ULTRAbots had found their way into my school. It felt like wherever I was, I had to look over my shoulder, especially now I knew the ULTRAbots could detect who I was at a glance.

I thought to the ULTRAbot I'd transported to the ice and the snow in the middle of nowhere. The one I'd frozen, then smashed and left behind. It took a lot to defeat it. To take it down. And that was just one of them.

They were too strong for me to fight alone. I knew it would take a lot for me to defeat them. A lot of courage. A lot of strength. And a lot of people. So I was going to have to hope I could avoid them. Keep as low a profile as I possibly could.

My life–both of my lives–depended on it.

"Kyle?" Damon said. "You even listening?"

I looked back at Damon. Everything seemed muffled, blurry. Every sound of a voice, every glance in my direction... It felt like they all knew I was Glacies. That the secret was out.

I knew I couldn't let that happen. I just couldn't allow it.

"Massive fight over Paris, anyway," Damon said. "Three ULTRAbots, four ULTRAs. Some of 'em firing flames, others firing live bullets outta their hands. Man, it was the craziest thing I've ever seen. Took the top off the Eiffel Tower. But the ULTRAbots won, of course."

"Of course," I muttered, a sinking feeling building in my stomach.

"What?"

I shook my head. I couldn't let Damon clock on to my disappointment about the ULTRAs being defeated. I mean, should I be disappointed that ULTRAs were being defeated? There were rogue ULTRAs out there, of course. Who were the good guys? Who were the bad guys? Was there even such a thing anymore?

I turned the corner, my thoughts and feelings still firmly rooted elsewhere, and I saw Ellicia standing outside my Geography class.

I stood still. Like I'd walked right into a brick wall. She was standing there, and she was looking into my eyes, with a half smile on her face. Her brown hair shone, and her eyes twinkled. I felt like I was seeing her for the first time all over again.

"You... aren't in my Geography," I said. And felt idiotic the moment after saying those words. I'd been together with this person for six months. Why was I acting like I'd never spoken to her before all over again?

"No," she said. "Nicely spotted. Hey, you've got five minutes, right?"

I looked at my watch, which didn't actually exist. "Maybe four. Or three–"

"Kyle, I'm not moving."

It took my brain a few seconds to adjust to what Ellicia just said.

"Well? Don't look so terrified."

"No," I said, my cheeks flushing. Shit. What was I supposed to say? Was this a dream? I'd prepared myself so much for this reality, and now Ellicia was staying? "That's–that's great. That's really great."

Ellicia didn't look convinced by my words. I wished I could sound more enthusiastic. Her staying was everything I wanted, after all. "Well, not totally great. Dad's new job fell through. All to do with the ULTRAs. Luckily his old place loves him, so they were happy to take him right back."

"So you're staying for good?"

Ellicia smiled. "For now. And for a while. I hope."

I looked down at my shoes. I felt happy inside, I really did. But a part of me felt afraid too. Because I'd accepted my situation as Kyle Peters. I'd accepted that with Ellicia leaving New York, I had less to lose.

But now she was staying, I had more in my non-ULTRA life to fight for.

Was that a good thing? Was that a bad thing? I just didn't know anymore.

"Anyway," Ellicia said, as my classmates starting jostling inside the Geography class. She looked down at the corridor. "I guess I just wondered if you wanted to go for a milkshake tomorrow? There's a nice new place opened right by the harbor. They do Oreo shakes."

I smiled. I couldn't believe I'd even questioned whether this was a good thing or not. "You had me at Oreo."

She walked up to me, then. She wrapped her arms around me, hugged me. And I felt like I was hugging her for the first time. I felt the warmth of her body. The softness of her hair. I still didn't ever feel totally comfortable, totally confident. But I was just happy to have her back.

But similarly, I was more sad—more determined than ever— that I had to hide to keep my life as Kyle Peters intact.

I thought about Bowler's words. About what he'd said about

giving up my life as Kyle Peters to take on my ULTRA responsibilities.

"See you tomorrow?" Ellicia asked.

I snapped out of my thoughts. Looked back at Ellicia and smiled.

"Tomorrow."

She nodded at me and walked away.

I took in a deep breath and headed into Geography.

Maybe things could get better. Maybe this was a sign that things were finally working out.

Maybe.

18

Mr. Parsons stood in the labs and stared at the body on the table in front of him.

Deep down here, underground, there was no sense of time, no sense of weather. It could be the middle of the day or it could be the middle of the night. He didn't know. Time was irrelevant anyway, especially when an army of ULTRAbots were out in the world hunting down the ULTRAs.

What mattered was he had one of them, right here. One of them he recognized. Not one of the ones who'd escaped Area 64.

Which meant there was something else going on.

He listened to the low hum of the fans whirring above. The lights were bright, flickering. He liked to be in rooms like this with the ULTRAs while they were strapped down and limited, of course. The knowledge that so much power rested in this room; power that had been repressed. There was something about it that made Mr. Parsons feel like a conqueror, like a hero.

But he wasn't a hero. He was just a normal man. A figurehead of the human resistance against the ULTRAs.

A beast tamer.

Or something like that.

The door behind him clicked open. He looked around and saw Idris leaning around the door, dressed in his white lab coat. He looked concerned.

"Sir? You um... You probably shouldn't be in here. Not so soon after we caught him."

Mr. Parsons turned around and looked at the ULTRA lying on the metal table. He recognized the blue outfit. The wispy hair. The boyish good looks. Spark. Definitely Spark. He thought this one was long gone. He remembered him from when he was younger, when they were both younger, at the tail end of the previous Era of the ULTRAs. He never thought he'd see Spark live to see this day. He thought he'd have disappeared long ago.

Never mind. He kind of liked the underdog.

"I'll be fine, Idris," Mr. Parsons said, keeping his focus on Spark. "Just a moment alone. Please."

He looked back around at Idris and saw his lips opening, getting ready to protest.

But then he just smiled. Nodded. "Of course, sir. I'll give you five minutes."

He turned around and left Mr. Parsons alone with Spark.

Mr. Parsons absorbed the stillness of the room for another few seconds. And then he stepped around the side of the metal slab where Spark rested. He walked slowly, heard his footsteps tapping against the floor. He could feel Spark's energy as he walked closer to him, and it excited him. It excited him like coming into contact with an ULTRA always did.

"I know you can hear me," he said.

Spark's eyes opened up the second Mr. Parsons spoke. He looked up. Looked right into his eyes. And Mr. Parsons saw the transferral of understanding. He saw Spark struggle at first. And then he saw him adjust to his surroundings, accept where he was.

Then, groggy-eyed, Spark looked Mr. Parsons right in his eyes. "The Devil," he said.

Mr. Parsons smiled at him. He stayed still, right by his bedside. "That's not exactly the nicest way to say hello, is it?"

Spark's chest moved rapidly. Mr. Parsons smiled as he watched him struggle to spark up his electricity. As he tensed his fists and tried to transport himself far away from this room. A breeze hit Mr. Parsons' face. The floor shook, just a little.

But that was fine. That was normal. That was to be expected.

"It's been so long, Spark. In fact, I don't recall ever capturing you. I thought you'd have gone by now. Thought you'd either have disappeared—the wise choice—or just... Well, I thought your powers must've gotten the better of you. Kind of spirited to see you lying here. Pinned down. Alive."

"You let me go. You're not gonna get away with this. We're gonna stop you."

Mr. Parsons held his smile and kept on looking down at Spark. "I'm guilty about having to do this. I really am. But I have a responsibility to the world to do it. You know I do. A responsibility to humanity—"

"You're full of shit."

"You know, we were working on the ULTRAbots for years here in government. Trying to find a way to truly harness the power of something as strong as the ULTRAs—stronger even—but without the repercussions of their actions. Without the potential for disaster. Anyway, we finally found a way, after much trial and error. I came along and gave the team an extra... well, spark."

Spark breathed heavily, tensing. Sweat rolled down his forehead. Mr. Parsons felt his fear like it was tangible.

And he loved it.

"So now here we are. I have your kind, both those who disastrously escaped Area 64. And others, like you. So now I need to ask you a question. A serious question. And you are going to answer. And even if you don't, I'm going to destroy all your kind. I'll make you watch your kind fall, I'll take everything away from you. And then I'll bring it all back and do it over and over again."

"You can't do that."

"Trust me," Mr. Parsons said, the first speck of anger creeping into his voice. "Don't ever tell me what I can't do. Not anymore. I'm here, am I not?"

There was silence between them. And Mr. Parsons saw a pale-faced understanding covering Spark's face. An awareness that this was it. He didn't have a choice, not anymore.

"So you tell me the truth. Who is your leader?"

Spark's eyes connected with Mr. Parsons' again. This time, he looked unsure more than anything. Conflicted.

"I don't enjoy doing this. I understand you are just ULTRAs, and there is nothing you can do about being ULTRAs. But I have a responsibility to humanity to keep people safe. And with aberrations like you around, how can I ever hope to do that?"

"Screw you. Screw you."

Spark spat right in Mr. Parsons' face.

Mr. Parsons didn't react. He just wiped Spark's spit away. Rubbed it against his blazer jacket. "There are other ways, you know. Other methods. Did you ever wonder what happened to Kal?"

Mr. Parsons saw the tears building in Spark's eyes. "Don't. Don't."

"We kept him alive for most of our experiments. And he put up a fight, bless his soul. Just a pity he was worthless in the end.

That the research we did on him came to nothing. Waste of life. But, ah well. He played a part in the creation of the ULTRAbots."

"No!" Spark shouted.

The ground shook again. Mr. Parsons felt that outburst of compressed energy rattle the walls.

He leaned in towards Spark. Leaned in close. "Then you tell me. You answer my question, or I will make your life and the lives of everyone you care about hell."

"You can't—"

"Your mother, Alice. She's a nice lady, isn't she? Does she know you're still alive? She still lives at the same place. Hell's Kitchen. Cute little flat. But you already know that, right? Because you hover outside her window once a week."

Spark's tears were in full flow now. Mr. Parsons knew he'd taken him by surprise. "Please," he begged.

"Tell me who your leader is. Tell me now, and we'll end this stupidity. Nobody has to get hurt."

Spark closed his eyes. In that split second, Mr. Parsons saw his spirit breaking. His resolve. "You won't hurt her? You promise?"

Mr. Parsons nodded. "I promise."

Spark sniveled. He wasn't a hero. He was just a weakling with some powers. Just like the rest of the ULTRAs. Take their powers away and what were they, really? Just losers. Failures.

Mr. Parsons' phone bleeped, breaking the moment. He lifted it out of his pocket, sighing. He knew what that sound meant. Another ULTRAbot transmission identifying an ULTRA. Another name to add to the list of captured, or defeated, ULTRAs.

But when he looked at his screen, when he saw the snow and the figure dressed in dark black looking right into the camera—the eyes of the ULTRAbot—he felt a twinge of fear and excitement, deep inside.

"Glacies," Spark said.

Mr. Parsons looked up from his screen. "What?"

"Glacies," Spark sniveled. "He's—he's alive. And he's our leader."

Mr. Parsons wouldn't have believed Spark if he'd told him that moments earlier.

But he couldn't deny what was on his screen.

Glacies was alive.

Glacies was still standing.

And he was the one leading the resistance.

He put his phone back in his pocket. Walked over to Spark's bedside. Rested a hand on his chest. "Thank you, Spark. Thank you ever so much. I'll keep an eye on Alice. Make sure she doesn't take the bad news too... well, badly."

Spark's face was normal for a few seconds.

But then it started to turn purple.

His skin grew cold.

His breathing went rapid, increasing but getting shorter and shorter as he struggled for life.

"Go to sleep now, Spark. Your duty is over. You'll awaken much better. Much more recovered. Much more... Heroic."

He saw Spark trying to fight as the life drifted from his face.

He saw the color leave his cheeks. Felt the energy in his body crumbling as he tried to fight back.

And then, he felt nothing.

19

I sat opposite Ellicia in Benny's Shakes and just like when I sat opposite her for the very first time, I didn't have a clue what the hell to say.

It was a nice day outside. The winter sun peeked in through the window. The streets were lined with snow, but not so deep that you had to trudge through it. Again, the snowstorm that analysts predicted to hit New York hadn't quite been as strong as they expected. Which worked for me. I had enough storms to worry about right now to have snow on my mind too.

The milkshake place had the smell of somewhere new. A crispness to the floors as you walked on them. There were quite a few people inside, as the sounds of milk frothing and glasses chinking together, as well as laughter, filled the room. It was nice. Somewhere I could imagine visiting a lot with Ellicia.

Because Ellicia was staying in New York. And I was staying as Kyle Peters.

"You like it?" Ellicia asked.

I sipped back my Oreo milkshake. Truth be told, it didn't taste much like Oreos, but I liked it anyway. And it didn't matter. The main reason I was here was Ellicia. The main reason I was *anywhere* was Ellicia.

"It's fine," I said.

"Just fine?"

"Well, the milk to Oreo ratio is a little off."

Ellicia rolled her eyes in a way that always made my heart melt. She leaned back, sucked on the straw of her chocolate and raspberry shake. "Trust you to bring ratios into milkshake. Nerd."

I caught the playfulness in her voice. It made everything feel okay all over again.

I looked into Ellicia's eyes. There were so many things I wanted to say, but I didn't know where to even start. I was worried. Course I was worried. ULTRAs like me were being hunted down all around the world. I had to keep as low a profile as possible.

But looking into Ellicia's eyes made everything seem okay.

"So yeah. I'm staying here for now. So you're gonna be stuck with me a little longer than you thought."

I tutted. "Huh. That's a shame. Thought my evil ploy to hire your dad over in Arizona was going so well."

Ellicia grinned, then kicked me under the table. "Yeah, right. If I'd really left, you'd probably figure out a way to *fly* to see me."

I almost choked on my milkshake. Then I realized she was still just joking.

"Anyway," Ellicia said, twirling her hair. "Are you..."

I didn't hear her next word.

Something smashed over at the other side of the building.

I flinched up out of my seat. My attention sharpened, honing in on where I'd heard that smash.

At the other side of the milkshake bar, a woman in an apron was covered in milkshake.

"Kyle?" Ellicia said.

I turned around. Saw she was looking at me strangely. And so too were so many other people. I wondered if they were looking at me because they knew. They knew I was an ULTRA. They knew what I was capable of... No. No, they were looking at me 'cause of how I'd reacted. I'd jumped out of my seat at a glass hitting the floor. That's all it was.

I sat back down. My hands were shaking.

"What's up?" Ellicia asked. She was looking at me in a way I knew I'd struggle to escape.

"Nothing," I said.

"No way. You're acting... well, you're acting creepy. And you've been acting creepy for days now. What's up?"

I looked across the table at Ellicia and I wanted to tell her. I wanted to open up to her about everything. She'd never been a fan of the ULTRAs, mainly because she saw them through the same lens as the rest of the world. But I had a feeling that if I told her, I could win her over. I could make her understand that I wasn't a monster. Being an ULTRA was... well, it was just who I was.

But I couldn't. I couldn't tell anyone I was an ULTRA. It didn't only put me in more danger—it put the people who knew the truth in danger, too.

And I wasn't putting Ellicia in danger any time soon.

"I'll be straight with you," I said, trying to regather my composure. Around the counter, people were still looking at me, whispering to one another. "All this ULTRAbot stuff. It just... it just scares me."

Ellicia nodded and sighed. "Yeah. Damon mentioned you weirded out when you saw the ULTRAbots the other day."

"You and Damon have been talking about me?"

"Course we have," Ellicia said. "He's your best friend. And

I'm your... We've been worried about you, Kyle. Especially after how you were after the attack at the party last summer."

I knew what Ellicia was referring to. The way I'd pushed everyone away after Nycto's attack on the school party. Really, that wasn't the reason I gave up and started moping. The real reason was that Nycto had hovered over Krakatoa and told me he knew who I was. And if I did anything to try and stop his reign, he'd not only expose my identity, but he'd destroy everyone I'd ever cared about.

I still felt the pain of those threats right now. The pain that hung around my neck everywhere I went as Kyle Peters, in everything I did as Kyle Peters.

"Anyway," Ellicia said, opening up her purse and searching for some more cash. "I wondered if you wanted to, like, get back together, maybe?"

I frowned. But it was more out of surprise than anything. "Get back together?"

"Well, yeah. Like, together-together. As we were. Remember?"

I sipped on my not-so-Oreo milkshake and let myself relax and smile. "I didn't even think we'd split up."

She blushed a little. Then I saw her smile back. I knew everything was okay again. I knew that all was going to be fine. Ellicia wanted to stay with me. She was letting me off the hook for the way I'd acted like an asshole at school the other day. And as much as I knew it was dangerous to be attached to someone right now, the thought of being with Ellicia outweighed all that by a million.

"Another milkshake?" Ellicia asked, standing.

I nodded. "Another—"

I didn't finish.

An explosion ripped through the street outside.

20

I didn't want to go outside. I didn't want to see what the source of the explosion was, or what was going on. 'Cause deep down, I knew. I knew damned well what it was, and what it was to do with.

But I didn't have a choice.

Everyone rushed out of Benny's and ran onto the street. Some of them screamed, fled their way home. Others stepped back inside the second they saw what was happening.

Across the street, a building smoked. Just minutes ago, I'd looked outside the window and seen it full of life.

Now, it was an empty shell. A burning mess.

And in the sky above, something was happening.

Something was unfolding above New York. Something terrifying.

"Come on, Kyle," Ellicia said, grabbing my hand. "We need to get back."

I wanted to move with Ellicia. I wanted to run. But all I could do was stare up at the sky.

There were ULTRAs flying around. ULTRAs *and* ULTRAbots. Both of them were engaged in battle, firing flames and ice at one another, shooting through the sky, ramming each other into buildings, into the ground.

I saw more debris fall beside me. Up the road, I saw a crowd of screaming people running away as this battle commenced. My kind. The ULTRAs. They were staging a battle against the ULTRAbots. They needed my help. They needed my...

Then, I saw something that froze my body to the very core.

A blast ripped through the crowd of fleeing people in the distance.

But it wasn't a blast that came from the hands of an ULTRAbot.

It was from an ULTRA.

I knew then what was happening, and it made me totally cold.

It wasn't the ULTRAbots causing the chaos here. They were just trying to stop something else.

They were trying to stop the ULTRAs attacking people. Innocent people.

"Come on!"

I ran a little with Ellicia, but I had no real sense of what I was doing or where I was going. I felt lost. Lost and confused. The ULTRAs. Why were they attacking people? What was any of this all about? Were the government right all along? Were ULTRAs the bad guys, and the ULTRAbots just the ones trying to do their jobs?

I ran down the street, debris falling beside me as more bolts of electricity and fire blasted past me. I dodged fallen people. Ran past falling buildings. I kept hold of Ellicia's hand all the time. But I didn't stop looking up, staring at the sky, trying to figure out what was going on and what I could do about it.

I saw something else happen then. One of the ULTRAs—a guy dressed in green who I'd seen attack that crowd of people just before—charging up a green ball of energy in his hands. He was free. There were no ULTRAbots around to stop him.

I felt my anger kicking in. The urge to go up there and fight him. To stop him.

And then someone blasted into the side of him.

I thought at first that it was an ULTRAbot, and I considered going up there and taking them both down—or at least away from here—while I had the chance.

And then, as I ran, I realized it wasn't an ULTRAbot at all.

It was Angel. The woman who I'd seen in the Pazza Notte restrooms. She was with some other ULTRAs too, all of whom were fighting with both the ULTRAs attacking the people *and* the ULTRAbots.

There was a war going on above me, and I was right here on the ground.

"Down here," Ellicia said. She started to pull me down the side of an alleyway.

I didn't go though. I couldn't. I knew as much as I wanted to live my life as a normal seventeen-year-old, I had a duty to protect not only people but the other ULTRAs, like Angel. I'd already let them down by allowing the ULTRAbots to take the ULTRA called Spark away. I couldn't fail them anymore. There was a time for sitting by and there was a time for acting. Right now was a time for acting.

"Run," I said, putting my hands on Ellicia's arms. "Seriously, just run down this alleyway and get someplace safe. I'll be back."

I ran away from Ellicia.

"Kyle! What the—what the hell are you doing?"

I stopped at the alleyway opening. I felt so guilty for what I was doing—turning my back on Ellicia. But I had to do this. I had a duty. I had something to do. "I'll be back for you. I promise."

"But—"

I ran around the side of the alleyway and then I focused all my attention on teleporting myself back home.

I landed in my bedroom. The sudden change to silence was deafening. Downstairs, I could hear the television breaking the news of the events. I could hear the explosions in the distance, too, muffled over here on Staten Island.

I had no time to waste.

I walked over to the cabinet where I kept my Glacies gear. I opened it up, stared down at it. I'd felt so sure about what I was doing just earlier. I'd felt certain that I had to put this gear on and I had to protect people.

But now I was back home, I just wanted to stay here. I just wanted to stay and let everything blow over...

No. There was a war going on. I had to do something. Even if I couldn't risk giving up my identity as Glacies, I had to do something.

I put on my black hoodie, my gray tracksuit bottoms, and a white skeleton Halloween mask I'd worn earlier in the year.

I caught a glance of myself in the mirror. Yes, I looked ridiculous. But I didn't look like Glacies *or* Kyle Peters.

That's exactly what I needed right now.

I teleported myself back to the scene of the chaos. There was an even stronger smell of smoke in the air right now. The screams were high-pitched and deafening. I heard approaching sirens and saw flashing blue lights.

I stood around the corner of an alleyway. Checked to see I was clear.

Then I looked up at the sky.

Focused my attention on the ULTRAbots.

I saw one of them flying towards the ULTRA called Angel. Pulling back its hand and getting ready to attack.

I lifted my hand.

Fired a spark of ice at it.

I knocked it off its course, and Angel went in with a massive punch, taking it out of the sky.

I turned to another of the ULTRAs. This time, there were two ULTRAs in a fight. A guy in black covered in blades, and the guy I'd seen fire the green bolts down on earth earlier. The guy in green looked to be stronger, winning.

I focused my energy and attention on him, and I fired.

He slipped. His grip on the ULTRA with the blades loosened.

The ULTRA with the blades broke free, and then he gained his ground—or air.

I shot at another few ULTRAbots and ULTRAs. And the more I fired, the more confident I was that I didn't have to become Glacies. I didn't have to make a show of myself to help fight. I could still be Kyle Peters. I could aid this war from the sidelines. I could...

Out of nowhere, I heard rattling. Like the blades of a helicopter.

The sky darkened. The screams diminished. The fighting ULTRAs stopped and looked around.

I held my breath. Stared up at the sky. Waited.

Then, out of nowhere, I saw them.

At first, I thought they must be some kind of migrating bird, there were that many of them.

But then as they got closer, flying through the sky, I realized they weren't birds at all.

They were ULTRAbots.

Lots of ULTRAbots.

And they were closing in on all of the ULTRAs.

I saw the panic in the eyes of the ULTRAs then, both sides. Saw some of them finishing their scraps, some of them disappearing.

One of the ULTRAs held her ground.

Held her ground and faced up to the oncoming ULTRAbots.

Angel.

"Come on!" I heard her shout, goading the ULTRAbots towards her. "Bring it on!"

I wanted to go up there and help her. She couldn't fight these ULTRAbots alone. I could freeze them. Or I could teleport her away.

But I wasn't dressed as Glacies. I'd be giving up another identity. I'd be—

My thoughts stopped.

The ULTRAbots swarmed around Angel.

I heard shouts. I saw blasts. A few ULTRAbots fell out of the sky. But so many of them swirled around Angel, getting thicker and thicker in number, like bees around a nest.

I watched and waited for Angel to emerge from those ULTRAbots. She seemed strong. She could do this. She could fight this.

But the seconds rolled on. The seconds became minutes. The minutes became...

The ULTRAbots hovered aside.

Someone dropped out of the sky. Hurtled towards the ground.

Slammed into the road.

The ULTRAbots watched for a few seconds. Looked around to check everything was resolved.

And then, as people gathered around the fallen combatant, the ULTRAbots disappeared.

I couldn't move, though.

I couldn't disappear.

Because Angel was lying in the road.

Completely still.

21

I lay in bed and felt sick with guilt.

I stared up at my ceiling as darkness filled my bedroom. Another shower of snow had arrived outside, the analysts now suggesting that a storm was coming after all. I listened to the silence inside my house, outside, on the streets, everywhere.

I couldn't close my eyes. If I closed them, I saw what happened earlier that day.

Angel hovering in the sky, waiting for the ULTRAbots to approach.

The ULTRAbots surrounding her. Swarming her.

Angel falling to the ground below.

And me?

I was just in a damned alleyway too afraid to do a thing to help her.

I tasted sick. My body was cold all over, even though I was completely wrapped in my quilt. I'd checked in on Ellicia, and she was okay. Shook up, and had a lot of questions for me, but okay. I felt bad for leaving her, but she'd made it. I would never have forgiven myself if I'd not only failed the ULTRAs, but failed her too.

I didn't know what to do. I didn't want to close my eyes, but I didn't want to be awake any longer. I just wanted this to stop, all of it. Four days had passed since war had been declared on the ULTRAs. Four days, which meant three days before his deadline arrived. The media were talking about a victory. Of ULTRAs being surrounded, taken into protective custody. Public opinion was way in favor of the ULTRAbots. There was even talk of employing them full-time to aid the police.

And to stop any remaining ULTRA that might be walking this earth, of course.

I wanted to reveal myself. Believe me, I was torn. I wanted to get back to being Glacies and get fighting. Avenge the loss of Spark, of Angel.

But I didn't want to kill those bad ULTRAs that'd attacked the humans. I didn't want to get tangled into a war that I didn't truly understand.

And I especially didn't want to cross the ULTRAbots...

I didn't want any part in any of this.

I closed my eyes, but they were burning so bad with images of the day that I opened them again.

When I looked up, there was someone standing at the foot of my bed.

It took me a moment to see who it was. The very same person who'd stood there about six months ago and galvanized me into action. The Man in the Bowler Hat. The one Angel called Bowler.

He stood at the bottom of my bed and stared right at me.

"What—"

Bowler pulled back his fist and cracked it across my jaw.

Hard.

I tasted blood in my mouth, but he swung at my face again. I didn't want to fight, but I didn't have a choice. I shifted myself across the room, dodged his punches, trying to keep quiet so I didn't wake Mom or Dad.

Bowler turned, fast. "It's your fault. All of this, it's your fault."

"Stop this—"

He hit me again. This time, in the chest. I crashed back against my *other* wardrobe—the one I hadn't wrecked—so hard that I was certain Mom and Dad had to have heard the racket.

I winced. My ribs wracked with pain. I shuffled up, eager to get to my feet.

Bowler walked across the floor, right towards me. He looked like he was getting ready for another punch.

"I didn't mean for any of this to happen," I said.

"You didn't mean it?" Bowler said. He picked me up. Lifted me by the throat with immense strength. "You watched it happen. Two of my people, trying to help you, and you *watched* it happen."

I struggled for breath. Gasped. I didn't want to use my powers right now. I felt naked using Glacies' abilities when I wasn't wearing the outfit, even if there was no one else around.

"You... you made me do this," I said.

"Do what?"

I head butted Bowler. Sent him flying back against my bed.

I flew at him them. Felt anger and pain and grief and everything.

My hands went cold. Super cold.

I held them above Bowler.

"You made me do—"

Another crack across the face. Only this time, a deafening sound ripped through my skull. A sound much like the one when I was teleporting.

When I opened my eyes, I realized that's exactly what'd happened.

I was in a dark container. Some kind of metal compartment. I could smell the saltiness of water in the air, so I figured I was by the harbor somewhere.

I stood up. My face killed, and felt swollen. I'd heal it when I got back. Bowler was in my home. He was in my home, he was dangerous, and he was going to hurt my family.

I felt something hit my back them. Something knocked me to the ground.

I spun around and saw Bowler crouching over me.

He put his hand around my neck. Lifted his fist. I tried to hold it back. Tried to shift away, but I was too weak, and he was too strong. He was like a reversed magnet resisting all the force I was trying to push into him. Whoever he was, he was strong as hell.

"P... please..." I gasped, gasping for air. I felt everything around getting blurry. Heard sounds that I knew weren't really there. Rustling. Breezes. "I... I didn't mean..."

Bowler let go.

He kept his fist raised, blood trickling from my nose into my mouth now.

"She died," he said, with a shaky voice. "Angel died. You could've saved her."

He turned around then. Walked away, towards the back of the container. It was the first time I'd heard him speak with any kind of emotion. Up to now, I was convinced he was something other than human.

I stood up. Focused an immediate burst of energy on taking some of the swelling from my face. One of my teeth felt loose. I'd deal with that in time. Maybe I'd look tough and cool if I walked around a tooth less.

"She was a good person," Bowler said, not facing me. That

fragility was still in his voice. "I'd known her ever since she was a little girl. She was... she was strong. But nobody is strong alone. Not against the ULTRAbots."

I swallowed a bloody lump in my throat. "I'm sorry. I was just..."

"Scared, I know. Scared of giving up your life. Scared of accepting your responsibilities."

"I'm just a kid."

"We're all just kids in this world. All of us. None of us ask for our responsibilities. None of us ask to be burdened with power. But you have a gift, Kyle. You have a very powerful gift. You have a gift that makes you significantly more powerful than any other ULTRA on this planet. And if you do not use that gift..."

He didn't finish his sentence. He didn't need to.

"You need to choose a path," Bowler said. "Right here. Right now. You need to choose which road you want to take. You cannot take both. Taking both roads is impossible. I'm sorry you have to hear that, but it's true."

Adrenaline raced through my bloodstream. I still wasn't sure how exactly to react to this. "How am I supposed to make a choice when I don't even know who the hell's fighting who? When I don't know what's good and what's bad? When I don't even know who the hell you are?"

There was a pause, then. A pause, as Bowler looked me in my eyes from behind that mask. I wasn't sure how long it lasted, but something about it made it feel like forever. Made it feel familiar.

Then, Bowler broke the silence.

"There's a good reason why I can't reveal who I am."

"Then give me the reason. Make it even. Go on. I'm standing here. You know who I am. It's only fair."

More silence from Bowler. For the first time, I started to

wonder if I had him in a corner. If the power was with me, after all.

"Go on!" I shouted. "Tell me. Tell me who the hell you are. Tell me why you were in my room. Why you know who I am. Why you think you're so damned powerful and mighty."

Bowler was still for another few seconds.

Then he reached for his head. Took off his bowler hat.

Underneath, I saw dark black hair.

"I'll tell you who I am. I'll tell you exactly who I am. Maybe then, you'll understand."

"Good," I said, as Bowler threw aside his coat. "'Cause if you don't, I'll... I'll..."

I couldn't speak. I couldn't say a word.

I could only stare at the man in front of me.

My mind raced with all kinds of thoughts and theories. I wondered if this was some kind of dream. It had to be. This couldn't be real. It wasn't possible.

But it was.

"Why... why are you wearing Orion's costume?"

Bowler rubbed his palms together. He looked me in the eye. "Because, Kyle Peters, I *am* Orion."

22

"You... you can't be Orion. You just can't be."

I wasn't sure what I said. I had no idea what words left my lips. I just stood there and stared at the man opposite me. The man dressed from head to toe in black. The man wearing the very same outfit I'd seen in the sky that day over eight years ago, planets and stars embossed onto its chest.

The guy that had crashed into Saint—sparked the Great Blast.

Bowler was Orion.

"I understand it's difficult. To accept."

I shook my head. My skin tingled. A bitter taste filled my mouth. "No. No, you can't be Orion. Orion's dead."

"Just like Glacies is dead?" Orion said. He walked closer towards me, his footsteps echoing against the bottom of the metal container. "Just like Glacies disappeared into apparent oblivion when he took down Nycto."

"That's different."

"How is it different?"

"I saw you... I saw you explode."

Orion looked me in my eyes. At least I thought he did—I couldn't tell because his face was covered completely with a black mask, not to mention the light being so dim inside this container. To think of it, he did look just like I remembered Orion. The Orion from the TV reports. The Orion I'd seen in the sky fighting Saint, protecting the planet. A little chubbier now, maybe. The suit didn't fit quite as snugly.

But it was him.

It was definitely him.

I watched Orion walk in front of me. I felt twitchy, as blood trickled down my blocked nostrils. I didn't know what to say to him. I was in awe of him, in truth. Here was the man who saved the world. Who sacrificed himself, and so many others, to protect humanity.

"What... what are you doing?" I asked. It was all I could manage.

"After The Great Blast, I knew I couldn't carry on like I used to. I was detested. I was hated. I was blamed for the deaths of a million New Yorkers, even though I played no part in the explosion."

"It was both of you. It was the power of both of you crashing—"

"That's what they have you believe," Orion said, walking from side to side, heavy footsteps echoing against the hangar. "But they would do, wouldn't they? They want humans to hate ULTRAs, remember. They want humans to hate us so much that they'll say anything to destroy us, no matter what. Kyle, I did not play any part in The Great Blast. I would not have made the move I made if I knew the destruction it was going to cause. I am still not entirely sure what happened, even to this day."

I was silent for a few seconds. Orion sounded genuine. And, weirdly, I believed him.

"Anyway," Orion said. "I pieced myself together. Saint and I battled for longer."

"The battle didn't end above Staten Island?"

"The battle raged on for some time after that. And in the end, it came down to two men. Two men so exhausted that we were stripped of our powers."

"But you killed him? You finished him?"

Orion nodded. "I did what I had to do. To protect all of humankind. All of ULTRA-kind. I am not proud of what I did to Saint. But it was the only thing I could. Just like you and Nycto."

I thought about Orion's words. He had a point. I wasn't sure how anyone could be guilty of killing Saint. But then I remembered I'd felt a guilt of my own when I'd buried Nycto at the bottom of Krakatoa, left him under the rubble. "Eight years," I said. "Eight years and nobody sees you. Nobody thinks you exist. Why now?"

Orion kept on walking, back and forth. "For the same reason as you," he said. "I saw the hate. I saw the fear. And I realized there was no place for me in this world. Not anymore."

"So you just hid?"

"I hid, yes," Orion said. "But eventually, I picked myself up. The government doesn't want people to believe it, but there are many more ULTRAs around the world than they'd have anyone believe. I spent my time reaching out to those ULTRAs. Trying to get them to understand what they were. To *embrace* what they were. To help keep the world a better place." He stopped pacing and looked straight at me. "I hid, Kyle. But I did not give up my responsibilities."

I looked down at his feet. A twinge of guilt flickered inside me. Because that's what I'd done. I'd been so focused on living two lives that I'd neglected my true responsibilities as Glacies.

My responsibilities to the world. "How am I... how are we ULTRAs?"

Orion looked at me for a little longer, then turned away, as if he was uncomfortable with the question. "We called ourselves The Resistance," Orion said. "We fought silently behind the scenes. Fought to keep the world a better place. But my influence was limited. My main asset nowadays is my ability to win people over to my way of thinking."

"So nobody really knows who you are?"

"Some. Not many. Only those I trust the most. My inner circle. Which is, incidentally, all I have left."

Again, he held that stare with me a few seconds, then looked away.

"My powers aren't what they were. They haven't been the same since the day of the Great Blast. Something happened that day. Something wrenched the height of my powers away from me. I felt like I was disemboweled that day—"

"Ew."

Orion ignored me and continued. "And I haven't been the same since. Which is why the time for standing up is more crucial now than ever before."

"The government," I said, taking a few steps of my own around this container in the middle of wherever. "Why do they hate us so much?"

"Would you like it if your cat started locking you out of the house?"

"I... don't have a cat."

"Would you like it if something that was supposed to be under your control started growing a mind of its own? Would you like it if your lights started flashing in the middle of the night? If your car started spinning around and driving all by itself?"

"It might help me pass my driving test."

"The point stands," Orion interrupted, clearly not a guy of jokes. "ULTRAs were Heroes as long as they were under human influence. And then they decided to grow a set of morals of their own. And then they became ULTRAs."

There were so many things I wanted to ask, it made my head spin. "Why do we call ourselves ULTRAs? I mean, I think of myself as an ULTRA. But that's something the government created."

Orion shrugged like it wasn't really a big deal. "Empowerment, I guess. Taking a derogatory term and using it as a compliment. Because we are ULTRAs. And we are strong as ULTRAs, no matter what they call us. It's a way of taking that name for ourselves. Claiming it."

More silence followed. Orion had a point.

"There's something I still don't get," I said.

Orion folded his hands. I swore he sighed.

"You're so focused on me, me, me. There's loads of you. Loads of you fighting the ULTRAbots, fighting each other. What's that all about? Why? And why do you need me so much?"

"You do not understand how powerful you really are, do you?"

"I, um—"

"Something is happening. A storm is brewing."

"You guys really like your storm analogies, don't you?"

"A war is approaching. A war not between ULTRAs and ULTRAbots, but something else. The ULTRAs fighting one another in the sky. You mention you've seen them. How do they make you feel?"

I scratched my head. Here was Orion, most famous ULTRA of all time, asking me a question. "Confused. I mean, I don't get any of this. But especially not that."

"Likewise," Orion said. "Likewise."

He walked closer to me. And then, against all expectations, he put a heavy hand on my shoulder.

"I want you to join us because I have the potentially misguided belief that you are the most powerful ULTRA in existence. I want you to join us because I want you to take my place. To use your powers how I would use mine, if mine weren't so exhausting to use these days. I want you to make this decision so you don't lose the people you love. Your... your family. Your friends. Your girlfriend."

There was such a sincerity in his voice. Sincerity I wanted to believe. "Why do you care so much about my family?" I asked.

Orion opened his mouth. Went to say something, then paused.

"Kyle, I..."

He just started speaking when something heavy landed on the roof of the container.

Hard.

23

I stood completely still as the footsteps echoed around the top of the metal container.

Orion was still, too. We listened to those growing foot-steps that had landed above us. My heart began to beat faster, racing with all the options, all the possibilities. Why would somebody be on the roof of the container? And what if it wasn't a *somebody* at all? What if it was a *something*?

"What do we—"

"Ssh," Orion said. And I did, straight away. Because unlike anyone else in my life right now, I felt myself fully trusting Orion. I felt myself believing in the power of this guy because I knew he was stronger than me. His powers might've diminished, sure, but he was the original fighter. The ULTRA who'd kept on battling for the good of humanity, even when humanity turned against him.

I had to put my faith in him right now. I had to believe in him. I didn't have a choice.

The pair of us looked up at where we figured the footsteps were. They moved backward and forward, over towards Orion, then towards me, then back towards Orion again. I held my breath like it'd make any difference. There was a groggy taste in my mouth, brought on by a lack of sleep. But I didn't feel tired. Not anymore. Exhausted with everything, sure, but not tired.

The footsteps stopped right above me.

And then there were no more sounds.

I kept my focus on the roof of the container. Waited for the footsteps to move again. But they didn't, not at all.

I looked over at Orion to see how he was reacting, what he was doing.

He was staring above, just like me. Waiting for whoever was up there to make the next move.

"I need to check it out," I said.

I wasn't sure where the words came from. Some place deep down that'd been niggling at me for a long time. But right now, stood here, I realized that I was going to have to start using my abilities more freely if I ever hoped to be safe. I couldn't turn my back on my responsibilities as an ULTRA anymore. It was scary, sure. Terrifying, even.

But I was Glacies. Not in his costume right now, but deep down underneath, that's who I was. That's who I had to be. Kyle Peters and Glacies, they were one and the same.

I had to start making a change.

I held my breath and started to shift myself out of the container, above it, so I could see what was going on.

A hand landed on my arm. Snapped me out of my trance.

It was Orion.

"Don't," he mouthed quietly. He pointed up. "If it's an ULTRAbot, they know. They know when you use your abilities. They hear it louder than a whisper."

I gulped. Looked back up at the container roof. Even though there were no more sounds, I couldn't escape the feeling that there was someone still up there, watching, waiting to make a move.

"Then what do we do?" I asked.

Orion didn't respond. Just kept his focus on the roof.

I wanted to go along with him. Believe me; I didn't want to shoot out of this container without a costume and start flaunting my abilities.

But I had a job to do.

I had to make sure the pair of us were safe.

"Sorry," I said.

"Kyle, wait..."

I shifted outside of the container before Orion could stop me. When I was outside, I saw I wasn't in a harbor, as I thought. I was right at the top of a scrap heap. Sitting atop a mound of trash in a tight squeeze of a container. Hell, I wasn't by the sea. Least I knew now why it smelled so bad of fish, though.

I looked back at the container I'd just disappeared from. Hovered alongside it, keeping myself camouflaged, even though I knew that didn't do much good with the ULTRAbots.

I held my breath as I rose up beside it. As I waited to go face to face with my assailant.

There was nobody on the roof of the container.

Nothing on the roof of the container.

I looked around at the rest of the scrap heap. Worn old sofas. Smashed-up cars. Massive containers spewing out trash of all kinds. Rats crawling around everywhere. In the corner of my eye, I swore I saw movement. People watching. People waiting.

I shook my head and teleported myself back inside the container.

"They've gone," I said, upon appearing. "Whoever was there has..."

My mind froze.

Orion was standing opposite me. But he wasn't the only one.

An ULTRAbot, male with buzzcut hair, stood right behind him.

He was wearing some kind of dry suit.

Powering up a bolt of electricity in its hand.

Getting ready to fire.

24

I saw the ULTRAbot standing behind Orion, getting ready to attack.

I wanted to shout. I wanted to tell him to watch out. To turn around. Someone was getting ready to attack him; I needed to let him know. And what could I do? I wasn't in my Glacies gear. I couldn't expose myself as an ULTRA. If I gave away my identity and my abilities to an ULTRAbot, then who knew what they'd do to my family, to the people I cared about?

That voice in my head was loud and strong as the ULTRA-bot's electric grew bigger, as I saw Orion start to turn as if in slow motion.

But there was another voice.

A louder voice.

A voice telling me that I had a duty. I had a responsibility.

And to hell with standing aside and watching someone else fall all because I was too afraid to give up my life as Kyle Peters.

I lunged towards the ULTRAbot at full force.

I slammed into it. Knocked it back against the wall of the container. I tried to shift us away, far away, but the ULTRAbot swung a heavy left hook into my cheek, knocking me back.

I flew through the roof of the container. Looked down and saw the ULTRAbot crouching down, then jumping up into the sky with me.

I dodged its first punch. Ducked just before it could make contact, that burning electricity so close to singeing my face.

I punched it back, right between its legs, as hard as I could. And then I bolted towards its head and fired ice into its eyes.

Electricity sparked from its eyes, and I fell back down towards the piles of rubble, the pain from the water conducting the electricity sending me off balance. I landed on the ground, right by a group of rats.

I was just adjusting my vision when I saw the ULTRAbot was right above me again.

It pulled its fist, which simmered with electricity, back.

And then it rammed it into my stomach. Hard.

I felt the shockwaves of pain. I felt like rolling over, like giving up. I wondered where Orion was. Surely his powers weren't so limited that he couldn't help me out here.

But then I saw the truth. I saw the reality of my situation.

I had to save myself. I was capable of saving myself.

The ULTRAbot went in hard with another punch. This time, I managed to roll myself away and disappear before it could punch me again.

I appeared above it. Grabbed its arm. Pulled the ULTRAbot back into the air with all my strength. I tried to teleport the pair of us again, tried to get us away, but every time I tried, the ULTRAbot just pulled out another move, hit me again, knocked me off balance.

Sparks ignited from its hand. It went to throw them at me; then I spat back at its face. I saw it sizzle, heard it yelp. Wait. That wasn't like an ULTRAbot. In fact, it wasn't even wearing the typical ULTRAbot gear, but more of a drysuit. That was... weird.

We traded punches in the sky, right above the scrapyard below. It was like a dance, only I'd never been any good at dancing, and in my former life I hadn't been much good at fighting either.

I felt myself gaining ground. Felt my punches getting harder. Felt my abilities strengthening.

I felt the anger welling inside.

I could do this. I could beat this. I could...

It was at that moment that I realized something.

This ULTRAbot. It wasn't an ULTRAbot at all. It wasn't looking at me with that same dead-eyed glare that the ULTRAbots did. It wasn't emotionless, reaction-less. It didn't even have that emblem on its outfit, which I should've noticed earlier.

This was an ULTRA.

An ULTRA was trying to kill me.

I felt the punch then. Felt the hard crack that knocked me off balance, out of the sky. I tried to hover. Tried to teleport myself. But my head was spinning too much. I was falling. Falling to the ground below. I was going to break my neck. I was going to slip into unconsciousness and never heal myself. I was going to—

I grabbed the ULTRA's leg.

Bit down onto my lip.

Teleported us to the first place I could think of.

The edge of the Staten Island harbor.

I held him down over the edge of the harbor. He tried to use his electricity again, tried to fire it at me, but I saw now that I was too strong for him. I had him pinned down.

"Who are you?" I barked.

The ULTRA smiled, blood between his teeth. "You have no idea what you're getting yourself into."

He started laughing.

I felt my stomach turn. Tasted a sickly combination of blood and phlegm. The ULTRA was laughing at me. He was laughing at me because I really didn't know what it was he was talking about. I really didn't know what I was getting myself into. That terrified me.

But I wasn't going to listen to his laughing any longer.

"Neither do you," I said.

I went to push him over the edge, into the water.

"Wait!"

The loud voice came from behind. I turned around, still holding the ULTRA down.

Orion walked across the harbor towards me. He was limping a little, and sounded out of breath. I had no idea how he'd followed me, but then again he was *Orion* so of course he'd found me.

"Don't do this," Orion gasped. "We do not kill our own. No matter what, we do not kill our own."

"He tried to kill *me!*"

"And he'll have succeeded if you kill him. He'll have turned you into something else. Something you do not want to be. Something you can never take back. Ever."

I looked around at the ULTRA, who was still laughing as he lay there. I knew what'd happen the moment I pushed him into that water. I'd seen how he'd flinched when I'd spat at him, the water sparking a severe reaction to the electricity. If I took his dry suit off and threw him into this water, I suspected it'd spell the end for him.

"You have no idea!" the ULTRA said, hysterical. "You have no idea what a mistake you're making." His laughter rolled on.

"Please," Orion said. "Do not do this. Do not go down this road."

I held my breath. Felt sweat trickling down my head. I wanted to end this ULTRA. I wanted to finish him, for he'd seen my face, and for that reason alone, he was a threat.

I pushed him back. Walked away.

"Good," Orion said, looking at me, as the ULTRA continued to laugh and roll around the ground.

Orion turned to the ULTRA.

"Now let's put you somewhere you won't come back from."

In the blink of an eye, Orion disappeared.

A blink later, he returned.

He stood there, a little steam rising from his body. He gasped. Put his hands on his knees. I could tell the teleportation that he'd used so seamlessly had taken a lot out of him. So much that he was coughing and spitting onto the ground.

"Where did you take him?" I asked.

Orion looked up. Walked over to me. Put a hand on my shoulder.

"Like I said. Somewhere he won't come back from."

The pair of us walked away from the darkened harbor as the sounds of the water rippled against the concrete walls.

SOMEWHERE FAR, far away, he kept on rolling around, kept on laughing.

"You have no idea what you're getting yourself into!" he cried. "You have no idea what you're getting yourself into!"

25

Mr. Parsons stared out of the window of his fifty-first story office.

He liked it up here. He liked coming here and looking out at the horizon first thing in the morning, watching the sunrise. Of course, in winter, it wasn't quite as spectacular; looking over the towns and cities and seeing a dim light behind the clouds. But there was something about it that he loved. Something about the way those clouds, just patches of water in the sky, could suffocate the impact and force of something as strong as the sun. The very thing keeping our solar system going. A pure miracle of nature.

He watched the sun rise and the snow fall. It was only going to snow heavier as time progressed.

He liked the snow, too.

"Sir? We've got an update for you, as requested."

He heard the sound of his intercom. Wow, seven a.m. already. He'd stayed here last night, just staring out into the darkness. Sleep was for the weak, as the old cliche went. The older he got, the more he knew that was true.

The things you could do while the world was sleeping.

The plans you could make.

The drama that could unfold.

He turned around from the window and walked towards his door. The marble floor squeaked under his black shoes. The walls were covered with all kinds of abstract art, something which stimulated him whenever he walked past. The underfloor heating was hot enough to seep through the soles of his shoes and warm his feet. The room was rich with the smell of almonds, a freshness to the air matching the crispness outside.

He liked his office a lot. So much so that he spent the majority of his time here. Especially since unleashing the ULTRAbots on the world last week. Wow. He couldn't believe five days had passed already. Two days left to keep up his end of the promise. To capture or destroy every living ULTRA.

If only humanity knew the next stage of the plan.

He stopped at the door and adjusted his belt, making sure he looked himself.

And then he cleared his throat, took a deep breath, and opened up.

Idris stood at the door. Now Idris had always been someone Mr. Parsons could trust. But recently, Mr. Parsons saw Idris looking at him funnily. Like he didn't recognize him. Like something had... changed.

He'd deal with that, in due course.

"What've you got for me?" Mr. Parsons asked.

Idris scooted across the floor. He was dressed in a white lab coat. His hair was thin and straggly. He looked and smelled like he needed a good wash. Just his mere presence was enough to taint Mr. Parsons' office space with something off. Something sour. "A list of all known ULTRAs in our custody, all known ULTRAs still evading our custody, and all known ULTRAs deceased."

He placed the three documents down on the glass table in front of them.

Mr. Parsons looked at the documents. The list of ULTRAs in their custody and ULTRAs deceased were longer than the list of ULTRAs still evading custody. But the evasion list was still pages long. Still way too long to be keeping to a promise like the one he'd made.

Idris spoke as if he could read Mr. Parsons' mind. "We aren't going to do it in two days. It's impossible. There's still hundreds of them. Thousands, even. And sure, we've got a lot of ULTRAbots. More in production and released by the day. But they're fighting back. They're hiding well. There aren't going to be enough."

Mr. Parsons considered Idris' words. He walked away from the documents, back over to his window. He looked out at the rising sun. It was burning through the cloud like a light in a forest. The snow was falling heavier.

"Sir," Idris said, appearing at Mr. Parsons' side. All these years working alongside Mr. Parsons and still he called him "sir." "With the greatest of respect, I can't help but notice you're acting rather..."

Mr. Parsons turned to Idris. Smiled.

Idris looked down at the floor.

"Rather what?"

"It doesn't matter."

"Rather what, Idris?"

Idris chanced a look back up at Mr. Parsons, who smiled back at him. "I don't know. You just seem like you're going through a lot. I just wanted to make sure everything's good, that's all. Especially with Kelly. I don't want you to mess things up with her. She's much better for you than your wife's ever been."

Mr. Parsons' smile twitched. This was something he wasn't expecting, and something he wasn't sure how to deal with.

"Kelly and I are fine," he said. He put a hand on Idris' shoulder. He felt his muscles tighten right underneath his grip, saw a glimpse of the horror on his face. "Now go on. I'm sure you've got work to do."

Idris shuffled away from Mr. Parsons' hand. Then he backed away from the room, towards the door. He picked up the documents with his shaky grip and started to walk away.

Mr. Parsons looked back outside the window, back at the sunrise. He liked this time. He liked to watch—

"Mr. Parsons," Idris said.

Mr. Parsons' smile twitched once more. He looked back around. "Yes, Idris?"

Idris looked at him with wide eyes. With a pale face. A way he'd never looked at him before. "When you say things are good. Between you and Kelly. What do you mean by that?"

Mr. Parsons considered his response. Waited a few seconds. "It means what it sounds like. Is there a problem?"

Idris visibly swallowed a lump. He shook his head, then took a few more steps towards the door. "It's just... it's just Kelly doesn't exist. I made her up just now. That's all."

Mr. Parsons didn't even attempt to hold his smile then.

It dropped completely.

Judging by the transition to fear on Idris' face, he saw it too.

The pair of them stood in total silence. The only sound was the clicking of the old antique grandfather clock that Mr. Parsons had bought years ago at auction. It was strange, standing here, both of them *knowing* but neither of them *saying*. Like a performance in itself.

"On your way, Idris," Mr. Parsons said. "We'll speak again soon, I'm sure."

Idris' face shook. Sweat trickled down his forehead. "Yes. Yes, we... I suppose we will."

He turned to the door.

Started to walk away.

And as Mr. Parsons stood there, back to the window, listening to Idris' footsteps fading away, he figured it was a shame things had to come to such a bitter end.

He looked across the room. Looked at the collection of ULTRA memorabilia erected in his office. Rares. Originals.

He looked at his favourite object of all.

Smiled.

Outside the office, Idris' footsteps suddenly stopped.

Something heavy hit the floor.

A struggle. A few gasps.

Then, total silence.

26

I looked at myself in the mirror.

The sun was rising outside. The snow was falling heavily again. I could hear the first signs of life awakening on the street. Builders whistling as they made their way to construction sites. Horns honking. The constantly audible buzz of Manhattan island just miles across the water.

As I looked into my eyes, I didn't see Kyle Peters anymore. Well, I did, obviously. I'd not had some kind of face transplant, or pulled one of those transformations that Angel did when she'd confronted me in the Pazza Notte restrooms. I wished I could, but the truth was, I couldn't.

But the fact was, I didn't see Kyle Peters anymore staring back at me in that mirror, because instead, I saw Glacies.

In the corner of my eye, I saw the flicker of my television. The news of an escalation of ULTRAbots. More conflicts and showdowns around the world. Two days remained of Mr. Parsons' promise to capture or destroy every single ULTRA in existence, whether the government knew about them or not. They were cutting it close. To be honest, I didn't have a clue how many ULTRAs were still left out there. I didn't know how many ULTRAs there even were in the first place. I'd gone from thinking I was the only one with these crazy abilities to a whole confusing world opening up before my eyes.

It was scary. It was terrifying.

But in a way, it was reassuring to know I wasn't alone.

Not only was I not alone, but Orion still walked among us.

I walked over to the cabinet where I kept my Glacies gear. A cabinet that I always got a knot in my stomach when I approached. I crouched down. Battled through the many lock and tightenings I put this thing in to make it inaccessible to anyone. My heart pulsed the closer I got to Glacies' gear. Because I knew what wearing it meant, this time. I knew what it made me. I knew what decision it meant.

A storm was coming. And I couldn't just stand by and watch it happen.

I opened up the last lock on the cabinet. The ULTRA I'd fought at the scrapyard filled my mind with dread.

"You have no idea what you're getting yourself into!" he'd laughed. I didn't know what that meant. I didn't know what was coming.

But I knew that Orion was right.

If I didn't fight, I was going to die.

If I didn't fight, everyone I cared about would die.

If I fought... sure, I could die too. But at least I'd be trying. It's not like I had a choice anymore.

I held up the Glacies outfit in front of me. Rubbed my hand against its smooth surface, feeling more and more sick as the moments progressed.

I had to do this. I had to be brave. I had to be strong.

I slipped into the gear. And as I put it on, I kept my eyes in the mirror, at my dark hair, the bags under my eyes. At my skinny frame. Because I knew I wouldn't be taking this outfit off again. This outfit was becoming my skin. This outfit was becoming who I was.

I was Glacies now.

Maybe one day I'd be able to lead a double life again. Maybe there'd be a time where the world would be safe enough for me to live as Kyle Peters. To have friends. To have family. To have a girlfriend. I hoped it would be because I wanted that world. It was the world I'd craved my entire life, and I felt bitter that I'd only had six short months to truly live it in a way close to how I'd dreamed it.

But right now, I had something else I needed to do.

I looked into the mirror. Looked at myself. I wasn't Kyle Peters in a Glacies outfit; I wasn't a person with ULTRA abilities.

I was Glacies.

I closed my eyes. Held my breath. Counted down from three, then remembered where Orion told me to meet him at seven a.m. if I really wanted to go ahead with this.

I saw my mom in my mind. I saw Damon. Avi. Ellicia. I saw everyone I cared about.

I'd be back for them. I was doing this *for* them.

"I love you," I whispered under my breath, tears marking the edges of my mask.

And then I slammed my hands together and disappeared to where Orion wanted me to go.

To my new life.

To Glacies.

27

Might be something to do with me being an extremely dangerous non-person with terrifying abilities, but wherever I went, I couldn't help the feeling I was being watched.

The alleyway where Orion told me to meet him at seven a.m. when we parted last night was still dark, but signs of light were emerging in the sky. The alleyway was hardly the kind of place I imagined Orion, the most renowned ULTRA of all time, hanging around. It smelled like stale pee. There were trash cans overflowing with rubbish. I swore I saw rats creeping along underneath them, reminding me of the scrapyard I'd fought off the rival ULTRA just hours ago.

I walked further down the alleyway. Even though I was wearing my Glacies gear and even though I was camouflaged, I still felt exposed. The ULTRAbots had changed the meaning of being camouflaged. They'd made it into something else entirely —something without guarantee. I had to be on guard at all times.

I walked further down the alleyway. Looked at the note Orion had slipped into my hand before he'd vanished hours ago. *Down side of Benash.* I looked up at the diner on my right, the

Wellington hotel across 7th Avenue, as Manhattan braced for another busy, snowy day. Definitely Benash. Definitely an alleyway.

So where was Orion?

I leaned against the wall to my right. Watched as the first signs of life started to creep past the alleyway, a day at work starting for everyone here. None of them looked down the alleyway towards me. But all of them had this weird look of fear on their faces. I knew why. It was two days until Mr. Parsons' deadline. Two days until the ULTRA threat was abolished forever.

I knew things weren't gonna be that easy. I'd spent long enough in this suit now to know when something was off. And something most definitely was off.

But what could I do? All I could do was wait for Orion. Wait for him to show his face.

Wherever he was.

I saw people in their windows above. Snow came down on me, cold and lumpy. And the longer I waited, as seven a.m. stretched into eight, as the streets got even busier, I grew more and more worried that something had gone wrong. Orion didn't seem like the kind to stitch me up. He had opportunities to get me out of the way if he'd wanted to. So where was he?

I walked away from the wall. Paced down the alleyway. Looked for a loose flag or some secret kind of basement entrance that I'd been missing all along.

I didn't find anything. Not a thing.

I started to worry then that something had happened. Orion seemed worried when I met him. Maybe that was just his way, but it wasn't beyond the realms of possibility that the ULTRA-bots had caught on to him. I wondered if he'd be able to fight them off. He was still strong, but his power had weakened. He wasn't what he used to be but he was still *who* he used to be. I couldn't think of a greater loss to the world than the loss of Orion, so I couldn't think about it too much.

Then, I started to worry that maybe I had been stitched up all along. What if that guy *wasn't* really Orion? What if he wasn't even Orion at all, but someone else? Someone imitating him? It didn't make total sense. If he wanted me out of the way, he could've done it in that container, or left the electricity-firing ULTRA to finish me off.

He hadn't.

But then, where was he?

I waited a little while longer, the nerves in full flow. And the longer I waited, the more uncertain I grew of coming here at all. I was stupid. Sure, I'd chosen to be Glacies, but not like this. This wasn't what I had in mind when I agreed to give Orion a chance in his Resistance, whatever the hell that was. This wasn't the tightly oiled army I imagined.

I went to walk away, to give up, when I saw something standing at the end of the alleyway.

I froze. Froze, from head to toe, as I tried to comprehend what it was I was looking at.

There was something at the end of the alleyway.

A large man. Seven-foot, at least. Dressed in a suit. Wearing a bowler hat. Long arms, right down past his knees. A completely pale face.

A blank face with no expressions, with nothing, other than some long, sharp teeth.

He was coming toward me.

28

I'd seen a lot of scary shit in the last few days, but this creepy, long-armed, pale-faced guy with sharp teeth in his boiled egg face? Yeah. He definitely topped it.

He walked towards me quickly, and getting quicker by the second. He was dressed in a black suit, and his long arms swayed by his sides. The hair on my arms stood on end. I tasted bitterness in my mouth. For some reason, this guy reminded me of someone I'd seen in my nightmares. A video game I'd played one night at Avi's that gave me the creeps for months and years to come.

And here he was.

I stepped back. I wanted to fight, but weirdly, 7th Avenue at the end of the alleyway was blurred like it wasn't even there at all. All sounds around me were muffled, like I was trapped in a bubble that I couldn't get out of. Suddenly, I became aware that I could only do one thing right now.

Get the hell out of this alleyway.

I turned around to run when I saw another of these men walking down the other side of the alleyway.

He was just the same as the man on the other side. Suited.

At least seven feet tall. Long arms dangling by his side, almost trailing along the ground. A pale face with no eyes, just a mouth full of dagger-like teeth, some of them etched with blood.

My breathing grew tensed and forced. My heart raced faster than I thought it'd ever done before.

I needed to get away. Quick.

I closed my eyes and tried to teleport.

A splitting headache tore through my body.

I gasped. Fell to the ground. My vision became blurred. The sounds around me went even more muffled. In my mouth, I tasted blood.

I looked up at the approaching men. They were so close now. They were shifting, glitching, like they *were* a computer game. Their teeth rattled together, click click clicking as they got closer.

I didn't want to go towards any of them but I couldn't teleport away. It hurt too much. So I was going to have to face up to one of them. Fly at them. I didn't exactly have a choice.

I held my breath.

And then I flew in the direction of the man on the right.

I threw all my force at him. Suddenly, I felt myself shaking off the pain that'd split through my skull just moments ago. I was Glacies. I was strong enough to handle these people, or whatever they were. I was strong enough to...

I fell to the ground, mid-flight.

I fell to the ground because of what I saw.

The man with the sharp teeth wasn't a man with sharp teeth anymore.

He was my sister, Cassie.

She stood there looking at me, tears pouring down her face. Behind her, the ground lifted into the sky, as a huge white light approached.

"Go, Kyle!" she screamed. "Get away!"

I wanted to help her. I knew it wasn't rational and knew something was wrong because Cassie was dead, but I wanted to help her, I wanted to help her so bad because she was my sister and I couldn't just leave her.

I tried to shift but I was stuck. Completely frozen to the spot.

I saw the light right behind Cassie. The light from the Great Blast, only slower than I remembered it.

I tried to drag my right foot along. Tried to yank it up, but it was stuck.

When I looked down, what I saw nearly made me throw up.

Mike Beacon was below me. He reached out for me, clutched at my foot. His face was covered in dust and ash, as well as scratches and cuts. I could tell from the paleness of his skin that he was dead.

But there wasn't just one Mike Beacon. There were thousands of Mike Beacons, all crowded down there, all reaching up to me, dragging me down.

"You killed me, Kyle," he shouted; all of them shouted. "You did this to me. You did this to me!"

I heard laughter, then. Looked up and saw Cassie standing there. Her face was covered in blood. Behind her were the two men with the long arms, the sharp teeth. Both of them were waving at me while Cassie danced on the spot, twirling like a ballerina.

"YOU DID THIS TO ME!" Mike Beacon screamed in a high-pitched squeal. "YOU DID THIS YOU DID THIS YOU DID THIS!"

Cassie danced.

The sharp-toothed men waved.

I wanted to fight. I wanted to get away. I wanted to be anywhere but here.

I knew I was strong. I knew I could do this.

But then I looked into Cassie's eyes, so far away, and I felt my grip slipping.

Mike Beacon dragged me down into the abyss below.

I was surrounded by darkness.

29

I felt my lungs fill with water, but at least I knew I was alive.

I opened my eyes. Tried to gasp for air. Someone was standing over me. Someone tall. A dark figure dressed in black. They were saying something. To me? I wasn't sure. But it seemed familiar. It seemed like I'd been here before; like I'd felt like this before, a long time ago. I wasn't sure what it meant. I wasn't sure why I felt like I did. I just knew I was alive, and that was something.

My eyes adjusted and I saw it was Orion standing over me.

I coughed. Sat upright and spat out stringy phlegm on the concrete flooring beside me.

Orion patted my back, hard. "That's it. Get it up. Get it all up."

I threw up on the floor. My head ached like mad. I wasn't sure what'd happened just before when I'd seen all those horrible things in the alleyway. I wasn't sure what they meant.

"It's okay. You're back with us now."

I realized Orion's voice was echoing. When I lifted my head, I saw that I was inside. It was quite a small room, with no windows. Just a flickering light bulb dangling from the ceiling, swaying from side to side.

But I wasn't alone in this room.

People stood around me. Men. Women. All of them... different, somehow.

As Orion patted my back and helped me get the rest of the phlegm from my chest, I saw what these people were.

"ULTRAs," I muttered.

"He's awful weak for someone who'd s'posed to be our savior," a man said. He was standing in the middle of the crowd. Well built, with a short buzz cut and bigger muscles than I'd ever seen. As I looked at him, I saw his hands turn to stone, then back to flesh again. He must've been in his twenties.

"Give him a break," one of the others said—a woman who shot around the room with radical speed. She had black hair and was dressed in white. She looked around my age. "We were all just scared kids once upon a time."

"But we didn't have a planet to save," another voice said. A guy, with a booming deep voice. He had dark, greasy hair and rounded glasses perched on his protruding bony nose. He looked a little younger than me, but his face looked hard, like he wasn't a guy to mess with. I saw blades creep out of his skin, like he was some kind of human hedgehog. If I hadn't already seen some weird shit over the last few months, I'd definitely have passed out right now. He looked familiar, though, and I realized I'd seen him—and the stoney guy—fighting in the sky when I'd been drinking milkshake.

"Give the boy some peace," Orion said, raising a hand. "He's been through a lot. I told you to go easy on him with the nightmares, Vortex."

I saw who Orion was looking at. A rather small, slight girl with long ginger hair and a freckly face. She can't have been much older than me, but she had a creepy look about her. I knew just from looking at her that she'd been the one to create those awful, nightmarish visions I'd had outside however-long-ago.

"I don't do easy," she said. "Just hard. And painful. You were interesting. You have a lot of guilt in you. I can read it like a book."

She clicked her fingers and I flinched.

"Ignore Vortex," Orion said. "She can be hard to handle at first."

I sat back. Leaned against the wall. My head hurt, and I couldn't shake the taste and smell of sick. "Where... where am I?"

"You're at our base. Far, far away from the streets of New York."

"Where, exactly?"

"You don't have to know that," Orion said. "Nobody does. Just meet where we met this morning and I will come for you."

"And if you don't?"

"Yeah," the speeding woman said. "We've mentioned that to him before too. Never listens."

"It's the only way I can guarantee your safety. And even then, it isn't an absolute guarantee."

I wanted to argue, to tell Orion that I thought his methods were shitty, but I didn't have the strength in me.

"Those things I saw. Why would you do that?"

Vortex smiled, and I saw her yellow teeth. She let out a witchlike chuckle. "Really got to you, huh?"

"We wanted to test your strength," Orion said. "It's all good and well having the physical ability, but the ability to face your nightmares, to stick them out and fight them instead of running away? That's something."

"I tried to run away. Believe me."

"But something held you down. A part of your resolve held

you down and kept you rooted to the spot. Even if you weren't aware of it, the very fact that you remained in that alleyway for one reason or other is exactly the sign we were looking for."

"Mike Beacon's damned hands held me down in the alleyway. That's all."

"Huh?"

I shook my head. "Never mind. Just... It's not gonna be a regular thing, is it?"

I saw a couple of the other ULTRAs smile.

"Believe me, kid," the guy with the rock-like hands said. "If it were a regular thing, I'd've been outta here a long time ago."

I saw some of the ULTRAs seemed to be chatting now, like they were accepting my presence. But others—like the man with the bladed hands and another guy with flames across his palms, also around my age—looked at me with disdain. I knew why it was.

"What happened," I said, clearing my throat. "To Spark. To... to Angel. I'm sorry—"

"Don't say you're sorry," a skinny woman with water dripping from her fingertips said. "You say sorry by action. Not by words."

"And Glacies being here right now is a start of that process," Orion said, the impatience clear to hear in his voice.

I looked around at the group. At Vortex. At the guy with the ability to turn his body to stone, the woman bolting around, the woman dripping water from her fingertips, who hadn't spoken yet. I looked at the man with the blades sprouting from his hands.

"Got something to ask?" the man with the bladed hands said.

"I just..."

"Go on," he continued. "Spit it out."

"Well, the Resistance. When Orion—"

"Bowler," everyone said, simultaneously.

I saw them all glaring at me, and I figured that even though everyone knew who Orion was here, we were all supposed to refer to him by his new name. Nice way to start. Way to go, Kyle.

"When *Bowler* mentioned the Resistance. I just thought there'd be... well, more of you."

A few chuckles around the room. A few shakes of the head.

"Well there *were* two more," the flamed-handed person said. I could see flames flickering in his palms, and wondered what destruction he could cause with them. He was young, too, about my age. Dark hair, pretty good looking guy in truth, a lot better built than me. He was wearing a leather jacket and a white T-shirt underneath. "And you kinda let 'em down."

"There were others," Orion said. "A long time ago. But this is all that's left of us now. All that's left of us to fight the ULTRAbots, as well as stop the rogue ULTRAs in their tracks."

"Those rogue ULTRAs," I said, standing now. "What are they all about?"

Orion shrugged. He paced around the room. "We have settled on the theory that many of them are ULTRAs who have been imprisoned in a place called Area 64 for many years. They have escaped, and now they are attacking the very people who put them in there."

"But that doesn't make total sense."

"Right," Orion said. "There is something amiss. Something wrong. Some of those ULTRAs, I've never seen in my life. All I know is they are dangerous, and we have to stop them."

"I'm about ready to put my damned fist through their faces," the rock-handed guy said.

"We don't kill," Orion corrected him. "We imprison. We interrogate. We do not kill."

A few grumbles. A few shakes of the head. "About time we

changed that rule," the woman with water dripping from her fingers said.

Orion walked up to me. Stood right opposite. "You have a choice, Glacies. A choice I have told you about many times before, but a choice you've held off making for so long."

"Because he's a frightened little flower." Vortex giggled.

"You join our fight. You lead us to battle against the ULTRAbots, who are our most immediate threat. We have been trodden on for a long time. We have been stamped on, attacked. Our numbers are low, but together, we are more powerful than anything they can throw at us because we have the power of decision and thought. We can fight. We can defeat them. But we need you."

I looked around at the ULTRAs again. This world wasn't for me. It was surreal. It was scary. It was unlike anything I'd ever had to adjust to.

But if I wanted to survive—if I wanted to save the people I loved—I had a duty. A responsibility.

I had to embrace Glacies.

"What do you say?" Orion asked. "Is your heart in this?"

I swallowed a lump in my throat. Thought about Mom. About Dad. About Damon and Avi and Ellicia and everything I'd fought so hard for.

And then I thought about what happened to Mike Beacon, what happened to Spark, what happened to Angel, and what happened to my sister, Cassie.

What I could do to prevent all those things happening again to other families, tearing more lives apart.

"I'm in," I said.

For the first time, even though he was behind a dark mask, I got the sense that Orion was smiling.

"Good," he said. "Then let's get started."

30

"This isn't going to be easy. It's going to take everything we've got, and a little of what we don't. It's going to break us. It's going to hurt us. It might well kill us. But it's what we have to do. It's what we're *here* to do. And if we don't do it, everything we care about will fall. Everything we've fought so hard for will fall. And I do not want that. None of us want that. So let's not let that happen."

I stood amongst the ULTRAs now, right in the middle of the row of them. Orion was opposite, pacing side to side, giving a speech. He had a plan. A plan he wanted to talk about. A plan he wanted to execute today. Because time was of the essence.

I couldn't deny I was feeling a little shaky, the taste of sick still clinging to my throat. When I'd agreed to join the Resistance, I'd expected it to be much like it was in the movies—months and months of planning signified by dialogue-free dissolve cuts into one another—*then* a foolproof attack.

But only an hour had passed since I'd agreed to help the ULTRAs fight against the ULTRAbots and we were gearing up for action.

I looked along the line at the ULTRAs. I knew all their

names now. The guy with the rocky hands called himself Stone. The man with the blades, Slice. There was Vortex. Aqua. Roadrunner. Ember. All of these people—these ULTRAs—and I wasn't just staring at them anymore, like they were different. They were what I was. They were ULTRAs. They were the last remaining troops of the Resistance.

Together, we were all that was left. The only force that could stop the ULTRAbots taking down every last ULTRA, and then tightening their grip on humanity in general, as Orion theorized they would, ushering in a new era of witch hunting, paranoia and increased security unlike anything the world had seen before.

"Roadrunner managed to locate a compound where the ULTRAbots are being produced. Now we are well aware that there are several of these compounds around the globe, but we believe this to be their main hub. If we can strike there, we can severely limit their numbers and make our job a whole lot easier."

"Cut 'em by thousands," Roadrunner said, still struggling to keep still, like a child after a load of Hershey's.

"Destroying the production compounds where the ULTRAbots are created means we have a finite number to deal with, not an infinite number. We cut off the head of the snake, and then we deal with the body. We also believe that the compounds contain the very power source giving the ULTRAbots their strength. If we can destroy that source, then we can destroy the ULTRAbots. We can turn this battle in our favor."

I nodded, tried to look sure about myself. I wasn't. Of course I wasn't. How could anyone be?

But now wasn't the time for worrying about what might be, of what might've been.

Now was the time for action.

"Every hour, Roadrunner observed that the ULTRAbots

switch shifts. Half of them go in for servicing and recharging; another half leave to attack. During that window, there's a ten-minute lapse in security where the ULTRAbots in for recharging are too weak to report any anomalies, and the ULTRAbots sent out are technically cut off from the main hub. We strike when the first half go back for their recharging. That way, they're at their weakest. Glacies will teleport us all there, and we'll strike as effectively as we possibly can. Subtlety would be nice—sneaking past these creations and destroying the source would be preferable—but we have to prepare for the worst."

Orion walked us through the Plan A. I teleported everyone over there. Roadrunner ran Stone into the middle of the compound, past the cameras and the booby traps, where he would change his form and take on all the heat from the weapons and the bullets. After that, the rest of us would make our move to sneak inside the compound itself, and in our own ways, we'd fight off whatever stood in our way. We'd battle through the ULTRAbots, who should be weakened. And then we'd destroy the power source, thus destroying the supply chain *and* every ULTRAbot produced at this facility.

"Any questions?" Orion asked.

Nobody said a word. There was something niggling at me, though. Something I felt the need to address. "Your powers," I said. "You said... you said they're weakened. Are you going to be okay out there?"

The silence around me reassured me that I wasn't the only one worried about Orion.

"Trust me, Glacies," Orion said. "I'll give it everything I've got."

He kept his stare on me for a few seconds. I got the feeling he wasn't so convinced by his own abilities anymore.

"No more questions?"

"Yeah," Stone said, his fists and body turning to stone. "Who wants a bet on who'll smash up the most ULTRAbots?"

"I'll challenge you on that," Aqua said, spraying water out of her palms so fast and so powerful that she hovered into the air.

"Me too," Slice said, sharp knives unfurling from his skinny hands, covering his arms.

I watched the rest of the ULTRAs reveal their powers. I watched them all standing there beside me, freaks like me. Except I was different. I had many abilities. Teleportation. Telekinesis. Strength. Speed. The ability to heal.

I'd never believed Orion when he said I was different; that I was special.

Now, I started to wonder if maybe it was true.

"Make peace with the lives you're leaving behind," Orion shouted, as the ground began to shake with the power rattling against it. "Say farewell to the existences you thought you knew. There is no time for sentimentality. Not anymore."

He put on his black coat and bowler hat, covering up who he really was.

"We are ULTRAs," Orion said.

"We are ULTRAS!" the group echoed.

"And we are going to fight for this planet."

"Yes we are!"

"Link hands, Glacies. Link hands with your people and do what you have to do."

I wasn't sure I was strong enough to teleport all of us away from here. But then I remembered I didn't have to be. Because Orion could teleport, too.

And the power in this room was tangible. I'd never felt more excited and afraid at the same time in my life than right now.

"Link hands!" Orion shouted, reaching for my hand.

I held on to Vortex's hand. Squeezed my grip around it as the rest of the group kept their powers charging up. I saw Cassie in my mind. Ellicia. Everyone back home who I was doing this for. The life I'd left behind to protect those people.

This wasn't for me. It was for them.

It was what I had to do.

"Hold on!"

I looked at Orion's hand. Saw heat simmering from it. A blue hue rising from it. I felt his power. Couldn't explain it, but there was just a feeling to it. A strength and a force to it unlike anything I'd ever felt.

I closed my eyes. Listened to the shouting, to the powers raging all around me. I felt the floor shaking. A tear rolled down my cheek.

"Hold on," I whispered.

I took a deep breath.

Let in all my anger, all my pain, every last bit of it.

Then I reached out for Orion's hand and an enormous explosion rippled through the room.

31

Paul Wilkinson always thought there was something different about himself ever since he was a little boy.

It started when they first got a cat. A ginger tabby called Brutus. She never liked him, even though he tried loving her, stroking her, giving her attention. She always spat at him, scratched him, like there was something threatening about him that nobody understood.

And then it turned out that *all* animals hated him.

Seriously, all animals. Birds would fly at him when he approached their nests. Dogs would bark at him, desperate to escape their driveways to deal with what they saw as a threat. Even flies bumped into him, like they knew exactly what he was and were trying to ward him away.

His parents didn't take him seriously, of course. They said it just probably meant he wasn't an animal person. But that was the thing—he *was* an animal person. He wanted nothing more than to cuddle up to a dog, to stroke a cat, to feed a little lamb some milk. To walk through a field of cows and not be chased.

But to this day, he found himself carrying the remarkable ability to turn even the most unintelligent creature against him.

It never struck him that it might be some kind of ability.

Not until he met X.

Now, aged seventeen, he stood in a dark cavern in the middle of the Scottish Highlands. He'd come here because X asked him to come here if he wanted to be a part of something. Just like he'd asked so many people already.

And Paul *did* want to be a part of something. He'd spent his whole life trying to be a part of something, trying to chase up his desires, only to deter people and animals away from him.

When X came to him three months ago, he told Paul what he was capable of. That he had a rare manipulative ability to shift the attitudes of the people and the animals around him. By default, because of his misunderstanding, he turned those attitudes against him.

But X had helped him hone it. Helped him focus his attentions.

And now, well. Let's just say he had a few too many cats crawling around his house.

He saw X at the back of the cavern, standing completely still. He was shaded, covered up, like he always was. Inside this icy cavern, biting cold, there were others, too. Lots of others. And as terrified as Paul was about being here with people like *this*, he couldn't deny that he was with his own kind.

He was an ULTRA.

So too were these people.

"We don't have long to wait," X said, his voice disguised by some kind of gadget. "In two days' time, the ULTRAbots will defeat what they believe to be the final ULTRA. Only they don't know about us. They can't know about us. I've made sure of that."

Paul knew what X referred to. The mark he'd given them, branded onto the backs of their necks. He claimed it carried a trace of his power, and he was *very* powerful. That mark acted as an on-off switch. A way of hiding in plain sight from the ULTRAbots that roamed the skies.

A switch that came in very handy, but would be unnecessary soon when the world was theirs.

"You all come from different places. From different backgrounds. Some of us have spent our entire lives with these abilities, fearful of what they mean. Others spend the last few years of their lives in prisons, which I helped you break out of. But we are all united in one way: humanity has robbed us of a normal existence. They have stamped on us. Trodden on us. And now they use *our* powers to create those ULTRAbots? To stand against us with our own abilities? Do they really believe they are stronger than us? How arrogant is the human spirit?"

Paul heard a few claps around the cavern. A few cheers. He felt himself clapping, too. X always spoke with such purpose. Such meaning. Such truth.

"This world isn't humanity's. Humanity had its time. Sure, they get their little short-term victories. They get their moments of peace. Their moments of calm. But they always just assume that things will get better. That things will get back to normal again. We're going to use that naivety, and we're going to take everything away from them."

More applause. More cheers.

"This world is ours for the taking. The governments don't know it, but the moment the ULTRAbots think they destroy that last ULTRA, we strike. We show them what we're capable of. What we've spent the last few months training to do. We show them that nothing can match our strength. Nothing."

X looked right at Paul then. And he felt his cheeks flushing. Paul knew what he wanted him to do. He could manipulate humans and he could manipulate animals, so he could manipulate ULTRAbots, right?

They'd tested it out. Tested it on one they'd captured. It was hard. The hardest thing they'd tried in their entire lives.

But right now, in this cavern, an ULTRAbot stood with them.

An ULTRAbot Paul manipulated. Trained to switch off recognizing them as ULTRAs.

They were hiding in plain sight, and they were going to use Paul's powers to turn the ULTRAbots against themselves.

"There is something else, though," X said. "Something... more personal. An ULTRA. An ULTRA I'm very keen on capturing for myself. An ULTRA who has evaded us so far. A dirty ULTRA who sides with the humans. An ULTRA you might've thought was dead, but I assure you, is very much alive. Glacies."

A hushed silence filled the cavern. Paul heard water dripping from the rocks above. Felt his teeth rattling against one another in the cold.

"I want Glacies for myself. But first, I want to take everything away from Glacies, just as he thinks he is winning. I've thought long and hard about this. I could've acted months ago, but I wanted to wait for the right moment. I wanted him to *feel* like his life was perfect, then to *feel* like he was strong again, and then I wanted to destroy everything he stands for. I wanted to wait for the right moment. And the right moment is now."

X hovered above the ULTRAs below. His dark shadow filled the cavern with even more darkness.

"You may know him as Glacies. But I know him by his first name."

X threw down a load of photographs. Poured them down onto the ULTRAs, hands reaching up, catching the photographs.

There was a mumbling around the cavern. Some whispers. Some questioning. A lot of disbelief.

Paul looked into a photograph and saw a young boy on there. Dark hair. Probably around the same age as Paul. Skinny. Smiling.

"The boy in the middle of the photograph is Glacies," X said.

The gasps filled the cavern. Paul stared into the eyes of the boy on the photograph, silent.

"And if we do not stop Glacies, we will not achieve our goals. We will not take the world for ourselves."

Paul heard more applause then. Then, stomping on the ground. Cheering. "Death to Glacies, death to Glacies!"

All this time, X hovered over the ULTRAs, shrouded in darkness. Watching. Waiting.

"Glacies' real name is Kyle Peters. He lives on Staten Island. And we're going to tear his world apart. Starting now."

32

I reached out for Orion's hand and an enormous explosion rippled through the room.

I thought at first that something had gone wrong. The explosion had been so loud, so violent, that I worried that maybe there'd been a fault in the teleportation. Maybe the combination of mine and Orion's powers had created something terrible and killed all the other ULTRAs in that room with me—the last of the Resistance.

When I opened my eyes, I saw I wasn't in a room at all anymore.

I was at the side of a hill. It was dark still, so I figured I must be over in the west somewhere where the sun still hadn't risen. Down the bottom of the hill, there was metal fencing with barbed wire wrapped around the top of it.

And at the other side of the fencing, there was a compound.

"This is it," Roadrunner whispered.

Her voice made me jump. She'd shot over by my side quicker than I'd even been able to take in my surroundings. I looked around and saw the rest of the ULTRAs here with me, perched in the grass, waiting to launch their attack.

"So are we going with plan A or can I get smashing some skulls yet?" Stone asked.

Orion sat at the front of the group. He was breathing heavily, like the teleportation had taken it out of him. He cleared his throat, then looked up. "We go with Plan A. Are you ready?"

Stone grumbled. "Rather not take a shit loada bullets to the body. But I guess I'm made of the strongest damned stone in the world."

"Good luck, Stone," Orion said. A few of the other ULTRAs patted him on the back as he stepped up towards the fencing. He looked at me and he didn't raise his hand to shake it or anything. Just stared at me, a look of cynicism about him.

"Don't screw up, kid. You got a helluva lotta people counting on you."

"No pressure," I joked.

Nobody laughed.

"Where is she, anyway?" Stone asked.

"Me?" Roadrunner appeared at his side, slightly out of breath, her hair in her face. "I was just scouting the area. Looks to me like the first ULTRAbots have left already. Which means the ones who've just finished their shift should be inside right now."

Stone stared at her with a frown. "You figured all that out, right then?"

"I told you. I'm super speedy."

"You're super something."

Roadrunner shook hands with all of us. Exchanged a few hugs. When she reached me, she hesitated, then opened her arms.

"Ignore this bunch," she said, as she wrapped her arms around me. "They're just salty they aren't as powerful as you."

"Good luck," I said.

She stepped away, went to Stone's side. "Hope we get a

chance to get to know each other a little better, Glacies." She grabbed Stone's hand.

"Me too—"

I hadn't even finished when I felt the kickback of Roadrunner's power, dragging Stone along with her inside the compound.

We waited for a few seconds. Waited for some kind of news. Some kind of signal that they were inside, and that the plan was starting.

"When will we know?" I asked.

Orion raised a hand. Held it there.

A blast of gunfire ripped through the total silence of the desert.

"Now," he said.

I did what we'd planned to do, my hands and body shaking with adrenaline. I grabbed Orion's hand, and then we all linked hands again, getting ready to shift ourselves inside the compound. In theory, Stone would attract all the attention his way. He'd trigger the ULTRA booby traps that were set up. Hold off a few of the weakened ULTRAbots while Roadrunner distracted them some more.

All the while, we'd go inside, destroy the power source and leave.

Simple as that.

"See you on the other side," Aqua muttered, as the rest of us linked hands.

"I hope so."

I closed my eyes. Held my breath. Focused my anger.

Then I heard that mini explosion again, and me, Orion, and the rest of the ULTRAs appeared behind the fences.

Being inside the fences brought a whole new meaning and a whole new reality to what we were doing. I felt vulnerable, all of a sudden. The gunshots were near. Somewhere close, I could hear Stone smashing things up, pieces of rock chipping away from his body.

"Bring it on, assholes!" he shouted, before smashing something else. "Bring it on!"

I felt a hand grab mine. Aqua. "Come on," she whispered.

I wanted to activate my camo, but I knew it was worthless anyway against the ULTRAbots and the booby traps, plus it took a lot of energy. Energy I didn't have to waste.

So I crouched down. All of us crouched down, wormed our way closer to the compound.

When we reached the edge of the container we stood behind, I peeked around. Stone was stomping around, taking the heavy artillery from loads of flying drones. But those drones kept on falling down every now and then, as Roadrunner played whack-a-mole with them.

"I can bring them down—"

"We don't have time," Orion said. "We have to get inside. The ULTRAbots left less than ten minutes ago. They'll know we're here soon."

I wanted to help Stone and Roadrunner. Even though they were doing a hell of a good job handling the situation, I couldn't help worrying about them.

I saw the entrance to the compound up ahead. There were cameras, electricity wired fences. We kept on hopping through the traps, hand in hand. Getting closer and closer to the compound entrance as Stone and Roadrunner continued their distracting mission.

"Just one more jump," Orion said. "Just one more, and then we're—"

He stopped speaking right away. Threw me back, and everyone else.

"Shit," Slice said. "What on earth was that all about?"

Orion raised a finger. Pressed it to his lips. And then he pointed at the compound entrance.

When I looked over at it, my body solidified.

Fifteen ULTRAbots stood by the door. They looked wobbly. Weak. But they still had that ever-present pissed-off look about them.

They were the ones supposed to be recharging.

They were looking right in the direction of the container.

I kept still. Completely still. So too did everyone else. I hoped they wouldn't see us. Prayed they wouldn't see us. Sure, they were weakened, but I wanted Plan A to work. I didn't want to fight them. I wanted to get inside that compound and get this done with. If I used any abilities right now while they were looking right at me, then I'd be putting everyone else in danger.

The first of the ULTRAbots took a step closer to the container.

"Bring it on, suckers!" I heard Stone scream, laughing as it sounded like even heavier artillery fired into him.

The oncoming ULTRAbots stopped their approach to the container.

Lifted their heads.

Then, they raised up and flew in Stone and Roadrunner's direction.

I let go of my breath. So too did Orion and everyone else.

"Got a clear path," Orion said. "One way in. We walk right in there. We can't use our abilities because we'll be incinerated upon entrance."

"Great," Aqua said. "Just wander in like we're going for coffee."

"Exactly. Are you ready?"

I saw the entrance up ahead. Listened to the chaos that was unfolding between Stone and the ULTRAbots. I heard metal snapping. Heard bombs exploding. If we weren't quick, the recharged ULTRAbots would be on our tails. We didn't have long at all. We had to do this.

"Let's go," I said.

The walk to the compound entrance was the longest most painful thing I'd ever had to do. But the closer we got, the more hopeful I grew. This hadn't been so bad. Not bad at all. The plan had gone perfectly. We hadn't lost anybody. All we needed to do now was get inside and destroy the power source. Tip the scales in our favor.

We reached the entrance and stared down the long, dark corridor.

"Al-right!" Slice shouted, clapping his rattly metal hands together. "That wasn't so bad now, was it?"

I went to take a step inside the compound when I heard something behind.

I turned around. Looked up into the sky. There was a low drone growing. Building. Heading closer toward us.

"What is that?" Aqua asked.

I didn't answer. But as I looked at the little figures moving closer—loads of them—I felt dread building up inside. Because I knew what they were. I knew exactly what they were.

"Are they..." Slice started. And then his face went completely red. "Shit. Oh shitting shit."

We all stood by the entrance to the compound and stared up into the sky.

An army of ULTRAbots—freshly charged ULTRAbots—headed in our direction.

33

I looked up at the army of ULTRAbots and, not for the first time since getting here, I got the feeling we weren't going to make it out of this one alive.

There were lots of them. Hundreds, all drifting in our direction. They gave off a humming sound as they moved towards us, like angry bees, only if we weren't careful, it was them that were going to be doing the swatting away, not us.

I felt my body shivering. Beside me, Orion, Slice, Aqua, Ember and Vortex all stood, silent and waiting. I could tell they were afraid too, as they stared up into the face of the oncoming enemy.

"I thought they were supposed to be far away from here by now," Ember said.

Orion shook his head as the ULTRAbots got closer. "Something must've happened. Something must've gone wrong."

"Then what do we do?" Slice asked.

Orion looked up at the ULTRAbots. Then he looked around at the rest of us. Looked at me, directly into my eyes.

"We do what we came here to do," he said.

He crouched a little. I saw a blue force field growing from

his hands, just like I'd seen so many times when I'd watched Orion on the television as a child.

"We fight," he said.

He jumped up towards the ULTRAbots. I saw him smash his fist into the face of one of them, and then move onto another, all of them engaged in a mad battle now to throw the first punch. He looked strong, but like this action was taking a lot out of him; like he wasn't running at max.

"Well," Aqua said, beams of water spraying from her hands. "No point standing down here."

She joined Orion in his counter-attack. Then Slice did, too, as did Ember, all of them up there in the sky, all of them engaged in this ruthless dance to the death.

"Well?" Vortex asked, a little grin on her spooky face in spite of the circumstances. "Aren't you gonna join us?"

She stuck her tongue between her yellowing teeth. It might've been the light or the angle I saw it, but I swore it was black.

And then she turned to face the ULTRAbots.

Her eyes rolled back into her skull. Her neck snapped right back. She let out a scream that sent shivers through my body.

In the sky, I saw ULTRAbots changing direction. Flying into one another. Becoming caught in whatever nightmarish trance Vortex was subjecting them to.

I didn't know what ULTRAbots dreamed about. But whatever Vortex was doing, it seemed to be working a treat.

I stood and watched the battle unfold. In the distance, I could still hear Stone and Roadrunner taking fire from the drones and the smaller group of uncharged ULTRAbots. I was scared. I was afraid.

But wasn't everybody?

I was here for a purpose. I was here for a reason.

I was here to fight.

I held my breath and shot into the air.

I flew into a crowd of three ULTRAbots. Slammed my fists into the first one's chest. The shockwaves reverberated through it, knocking three more down with it.

I saw an ULTRAbot flying towards my left. It was close. Really close.

But I just kept my anger at the surface.

Focused on shifting around it. Teleporting behind it.

And then I sent a blast of ice down its spine and froze it in mid-air.

I fought off more of the ULTRAbots. And after a while of fighting, timing my punches just right, making my moves at the perfect opportunities, I felt like I was in a flow state. Like I was invincible. Like no matter what happened, I could fight off these things; these enemies. Because I was Glacies. I was strong. And I could take on anything.

And then I saw five ULTRAbots surrounding Slice and Ember, swarming around them.

And another three holding Aqua up by both her arms.

Down on the ground, six ULTRAbots all flying towards Vortex, dodging her nightmarish trance-induction.

I knew I couldn't save all of them. I could use some help from Orion, but he was already well engaged in battle. I could maybe save one of them, if I were lucky. But I wasn't strong or quick enough to...

No.

No, I *was* strong enough. I *was* quick enough.

I could do this. I had to do this.

I felt time slow down around me. Felt the battle between a hundred ULTRAbots and a small group of ULTRAs come to a sudden, jarring standstill.

I teleported over to Slice and Ember. Clapped my hands

together and sent a blast of ice flying up into the faces of the ULTRAbots surrounding them.

I pushed one of the ULTRAbots down towards the ground. Hard. Watched its lifeless body fly in the direction of Vortex.

And then I pulled out my hands. Sent two blasts of ice to over towards the ULTRAbots holding on to Aqua.

Time still moved slowly. Infinitely.

And then it sped up to normal speed.

The blast of ice I'd fired around Slice and Ember blew up into the ULTRAbots' faces.

The ULTRAbot I'd thrown to the ground hit Vortex, knocked her out of the way of the oncoming ULTRAbots.

When they smashed against the ground, I focused all my energy and felt something opening up. Something like my tele-portation. And then I realized, as a ripping sensation crossed my chest, that I'd opened up a wormhole using a deep strength I didn't even know I had. Another depth to my powers.

I sent the ULTRAbots flying down towards Vortex through it.

And then I rushed over to Aqua. Slammed my fist into the backs of each of the ULTRAbots and sent them shooting out into the sky.

I saw Aqua look at me, amazement in her eyes. She didn't say thanks. She just nodded.

Slice did, too. Looked at me, baffled. But I knew I'd earned my stripes. I knew I'd earned their respect, just for that move.

"I'll make you regret putting me on my ass someday," Vortex shouted.

I looked down. Smiled. "Yeah, I think you've already punished me enough—"

Something slammed into my side.

Sent me flying down to the ground.

My back cracked against the solid concrete below. When I

looked up, I saw that my fellow ULTRAs were surrounded again, caught in the throes of battle. I was alone down here. They had no time to help me.

Standing above me, the biggest ULTRAbot I'd ever seen.

And he was holding a gun to my head.

34

I looked up into the gun and waited for it to blast through my skull.

I closed my eyes. Held my breath. Tried to shift out of the way. But it was worthless. The ULTRAbot above me was holding me down, suppressing my powers in some way. Or perhaps it was something to do with the force I'd hit the ground. My back ached. I could taste blood. The smell of smoke filled the air as the sounds of battle above rallied on.

I couldn't move. I couldn't break free.

This was it.

I saw my family flash before my eyes. Saw Mom and Dad. I saw Ellicia, Avi, Damon. And I saw my sister, Cassie, too. I knew I'd be with her soon. I didn't want to fail her, but I wasn't strong enough for this. I wasn't strong enough to be Glacies. The ULTRAbots, they were too powerful. Nobody could stop them. It was just a horrible reality I had to accept.

I opened my eyes and saw the ULTRAbot was gone.

In its place, Vortex.

She grinned at me. And this time, as she chuckled, I really did see her blackened tongue, her yellow-toothed smile.

"Told you I'd get you back," she said.

I wanted to jump up there and throw her miles away from here. But I couldn't because I was relieved as it was. In the distance, I could still see the rest of the ULTRAs, Orion included, fighting away in the sky.

"Now's not the time for that shit," I said, standing up and dusting myself off.

"You're only saying that 'cause you're blushing under that little mask of yours."

"Is that the thanks I get for saving you?"

Vortex raised her hands. I noticed her long unpainted fingernails then. "Hey. You put me on my ass at the hands of an ULTRAbot, I figured I'd better return the favor. Now hurry up. You've got a job to do."

She patted me on the back, and it was only then that I realized what job Vortex referred to.

The doorway to the ULTRAbot facility was open. Wide open, waiting for someone to go inside and do what we came here to do.

Reach the switch.

Shut down the ULTRAbots.

I heard a blast up above. When I looked up, I saw Orion. He was surrounded by ULTRAbots. I was in awe of him. He moved just like he used to move, only slightly more sluggish, his actions more forced and pained. But I still couldn't believe this was him. This was actually him, and I was here fighting for him.

No, not *for* him. *With* him.

I turned back to the door. Took a deep breath as the battle in the sky raged on.

Then, I stepped inside.

The corridor was long and dark. There was a total stillness about this place. So still that it was impossible to believe there was chaos unfolding outside.

I kept my footsteps slow. And even though I knew the ULTRAbots could see through it, I stayed camouflaged, too. It just gave me an extra layer of security. For my own peace of mind, more than anything.

I walked down the corridor. The doors to my left were made of solid metal. The windows were tinted. I had no idea what was inside, but it felt like there was something living in there.

I wasn't sure I wanted to see it for myself.

I kept on walking down the corridor. Every step I took, the more it felt like I was being watched, the more it seemed like I was walking into a trap. I kept my breathing cool, as sweat rolled down my face under my mask. Every little movement in the darkness, my eyes picked up on, even if they weren't there.

I went to turn the corner when I saw three ULTRAbots standing there, looking right at me.

I jolted back. Pressed up against the wall. Had they seen me? I couldn't hear them, so maybe they hadn't. Maybe I was okay. Damn, I hoped I was okay.

I swallowed a lump in my throat and edged closer towards the side of the wall. The ULTRAbots looked even more stationary and rooted to the spot than the ones outside. They were holding heavy guns, too. Like, really heavy. The kinds of guns I didn't think it was possible for a human frame to hold on to.

But then these weren't humans, were they?

I peeked around the side of the corner at them.

One of the guns was pointed right at me.

It fired.

I jumped out of the way just in time. And it was a damned good job because whatever ammunition was in those rifles, it blasted a hole in the corridor wall opposite.

I heard the footsteps coming towards me then. I knew I needed to get past them. Not just that, but I had to deal with them. I had to get rid of them or they'd never stop hunting me down.

I waited until the ULTRAbots' footsteps were just inches around the side of the corner.

Then I shifted through the wall.

Right behind them.

I put my hands on the back of one of them.

Immediately, the other two turned.

Pointed their guns at me.

I let out a cry as I forced the largest blast of power I'd ever created.

But that didn't stop me.

I'd created two wormholes right in front of each of the ULTRAbots. Two wormholes that led out through the walls behind the ULTRAbots.

So the bullets just flew through the ULTRAbots.

Flew from one gun, and then out of the wormhole in the wall, and into the ULTRAbots' backs.

I flew back with the force of the explosion as it ripped through the corridor. I lay there, looked at the flames, gasping for air. Whatever I'd done with that wormhole thing, it was definitely the most power-taxing ability in my locker. I felt exhausted. All out of fight.

But I had to keep on going.

I limped further down the corridor. And as I moved, it seemed to narrow. Curve. Steps appeared below me, but it all led in one direction. And once again, I started to consider that maybe this was some kind of trap. Some kind of tunnel that led to nowhere.

And then I saw it.

It was quite comical, really. So comical that it made me smile. When Orion told me there was a switch-off button rumored to be inside this place, something powering the

ULTRAbots, I didn't *literally* think he meant a switch-off button.

But there it was. A big, red button, flashing light.

By its side, loads of empty containers, like the ones rich people are frozen in when they die. Some of them were empty. But others were sprouting new life. New ULTRAbot life.

I tried not to look at the containers. It was too creepy. I just walked over to that red button. Hovered my hand over it.

I knew what I was doing if I committed this action. I was ending the potential lives of thousands of ULTRAbots. I was officially committing a terrorist act—an act that would turn humanity against Glacies for good, no matter how unfounded that was.

But was it unfounded? I'd seen what ULTRAs could do. I'd seen how dangerous they could be.

Was I being selfish by destroying these ULTRAbots?

Was I really thinking about humanity, or was I thinking about myself?

I breathed in deeply. Looked down at row upon row of chambers, at all the potential life they held.

No. I was doing this for the future. For the future of ULTRAs, and the future of humanity.

I was doing this for the right reason.

I took another deep breath.

Then I pressed down on the red button.

Hard.

35

A qua had never trusted the new ULTRA on the block called Glacies. Not really.

But after he'd saved her from almost certain destruction at the hands of an ULTRAbot not long ago, well, her opinion of him might just have changed.

Just a little.

The ULTRAbots were still in full force. Aqua raised her hands whenever one of them came near her, sent a strong blast of water right into them. It wasn't just any old splash of water. It was a powerful punch that Aqua had first discovered just three years ago while in the shower. She'd been convinced it was something to do with a burst pipe at first. And then she considered the possibility she was haunted or possessed.

It was Bowler who finally convinced her that she had the abilities of an ULTRA, and that ULTRAs were very much alive in the world. Alive, and required more than ever.

"Where the hell's he at?" Slice shouted.

Aqua looked and saw Slice cutting the ULTRAbots out of the sky. There were still so many of them, their bodies droning on like killer bees. Aqua wasn't sure what'd gone wrong for all these fully charged ULTRAbots to reach their position, but the 'what' honestly didn't matter so much anymore. It was the way things were, and it's just something they had to deal with.

"He'll come through," Bowler said. He bolted between two ULTRAbots, sent them crashing into one another, malfunctioning on the spot.

It was good to see Bowler fighting like he supposedly used to during his Orion days. But there was something sad about it, too. Something bittersweet. After all, he didn't look at his strongest. He had to take a moment to gasp, to catch his breath, whenever he took down an ULTRAbot.

But he was fighting. He was their leader, and he was fighting. Aqua wasn't sure what it was about Glacies that awakened this new determined focus and drive in him. Sure, Glacies was powerful, but this seemed like something more. Something deeper.

Whatever it was, it had to be good news.

"Just be patient," Bowler shouted, hands on his knees. "He'll come through."

The wave of ULTRAbots was never-ending. It seemed like, for every one they fought off, another two arrived in their place. Aqua wasn't sure how long she could go on like this. She could see the exhaustion on Vortex's face too, as well as Ember's, Slice's, Stone's and Roadrunner's, who had joined them in the greater battle now. There was only so long they could fight. Only so long they could hold on. Right now, they were faced with one of two certainties—death, or victory.

And it didn't look like the odds were stacking in victory's favor.

"I wish he'd hurry up, whatever he's doing," Aqua cried as she dodged the extended spear of an ULTRAbot, blasted water into its face.

And then she felt a sharp pain on her left side.

"Agh!"

She felt herself tumbling. Tumbling to the ground below. But when she looked down, she didn't see the ground. She saw a carpet of ULTRAbots. A carpet of ULTRAbots waiting for her to fall, getting ready to drag her away from here.

She tried to fire water at them, but the pain on her side made her too weak, made the process too hard. So she kept on falling. Kept on falling down to this mass of ULTRAbots below.

She closed her eyes. She couldn't beg anyone to help her. They'd helped her enough these last few years.

She'd lost her battle. She was going to be taken away, and then that'd just be the start.

Glacies had failed.

Glacies had...

She saw something strange.

The ULTRAbots below her lowered their heads.

Fell to their knees.

And then before she knew it, as she fell onto their stationary bodies, she saw the rest of the ULTRAbots above no longer engaged in battle. Falling from the dark sky to the ground below.

"He... he did it," Aqua mumbled.

"He really god-damned did it," Stone shouted.

The group of them watched as the ULTRAbots, hundreds of them, rained down onto the ground below. They watched as they hit the hard concrete. As their bodies went still, like they'd never had any life in them at all.

And despite the pain in Aqua's side, she couldn't help smiling.

She couldn't help cheering.

Glacies really was their hero after all.

36

When I heard the muffled cries outside the compound, I knew the off switch had worked.

I turned around from it and walked away, a spring in my step. Another reason I knew the ULTRAbots in here were dead? The whirring noise I'd heard earlier had faded completely. The ULTRAbots being produced and charged in these cryogenic-like containers had suddenly lost their rigidity, a murkiness building in the water around them.

I felt a shred of guilt for them. Sure, they weren't humans, and they weren't ULTRAs. In fact, they were practically robotic. But they'd been tools. Tools used in a war to hunt down my kind. They had no say in what they did. They had no power, not really.

I'd done what I had to do. And as grim as it was, as hard as it was to carry out, I'd done the right thing.

I walked out of the massive ULTRAbot breeding room beneath the compound. Climbed back up the stairs, towards the corridor where I'd fought off the gun-toting ULTRAbots not long ago. I walked down the darkened corridor towards the door, the way out. I wondered what the rest of the Resistance would be like with me after this? Surely they'd be happy with me. I'd proven myself. Done myself proud, I hoped.

Just had to pray Vortex didn't leave me on my ass again.

I was about to step out of the door and into the grounds of the compound when I noticed something.

The door on my right was open. The steel door with the tinted windows.

I swore I could hear mumbling coming from inside.

I turned around. Walked over to it, slowly. Triggering the switch must've opened it up. As I got closer to it, I smelled something remarkably like sweat. Human sweat. Just like before, when I'd sensed something was alive in here, I felt that worry again.

I should just walk away. I should just turn around and leave.

But I couldn't, because I wanted to see what it was.

I reached the door. Pushed it open. I tried to move it gently, but it was rock solid, so I applied a little extra force with the help of my ULTRA abilities.

When the door opened, I saw a large room. It was like a medical experimentation room, with a table and metal slab in the middle of it. There was nobody on there. But I couldn't shake the feeling that someone had been there at some stage.

All around the room was medical equipment. Medicines. Tools. All kinds of devices that scared me. I wondered what people had been through in here. What they'd been through to make the ULTRAbots possible.

Whatever it was, I didn't want to stay in here anymore.

I went to step away when I heard the muffled voice again.

It froze me, right there. Made me stop dead in my tracks. There was somebody in here. Someone, or something.

I looked around. Tried to figure out where the voice came from.

And then I saw it.

The metal locker door at the other side of the room.

Again, I wanted to walk away. I wanted to leave this place. Whatever was behind that door could not be good news.

But I had to know what it was. I couldn't just disappear. Not now.

I moved slowly towards it. And as I got closer, I saw I could just pull that handle using my telekinesis from afar. I'd just been delaying the inevitable, that I was going to have to open it at some stage or other.

I stopped a few meters from the door. My heart pounded, and I heard my pulse racing. I cleared my dry throat. Lifted my hand. I needed to know what was in there. I needed to see.

I pulled the door open.

When I saw what was in there, I nearly ran the hell away from this place.

It was a man. A man with long, dark hair, bearded. And he wasn't in a locker at all. No, the space behind the cupboard was a little white-tiled room. In there, I saw a toilet, which explained the smell. Stacks of dishes as high as the man himself, dirty and uncleaned.

The man was dressed in a suit, but it looked way too baggy on his frame. His lips quivered, as he looked at me with blood-shot eyes.

"What..." I started.

And then it clicked.

As this man stumbled out of this room, his legs weak and shaky, I looked past the beard, past the gauntness of his face.

I saw who it was.

This man was Mr. Parsons. The same man who'd declared an ULTRAbot war against the remaining ULTRAs. Who promised to destroy every last ULTRA in two days time.

But it couldn't be. He couldn't look so different in the space of a week. It couldn't be the same person.

Could it?

"My wife," Mr. Parsons gasped. He dropped to his knees, tears rolling down his face. "Haven't—haven't seen her. Three whole years. Three wholey-moley years. Please take me to her. Don't let the bad man in the suit get me again. Don't let him!"

"You've been here three years?"

"Three whole years and a moon after moon. In here, he tells me. In here, at the top of his voice, my wife! My wife!"

I listened to the hysterical ramblings of Mr. Parsons—undeniably Mr. Parsons—and a sense of dread built up inside me.

"The... the ULTRAbots," I said. "All of this. You don't know anything about it?"

He looked at me with bleary-eyed terror and insanity. I took that as my answer.

I felt the nerves growing. Felt myself feeling dizzy and sick. One question spun around my mind. One question that I feared I wouldn't really like the answer to. One question that changed everything.

If this was Mr. Parsons, which it clearly was, then who was the man pretending to be him?

Who was the man behind the ULTRAbots?

37

M r. Parsons stared at the scenes of chaos on the news and he smiled.

He'd expected his plan to go perfectly. After all, he'd been plotting it for years, ever since he disappeared into the shadows. But this good? No. He never thought it would go this good.

He took a sip of strong brandy as he stood in his office, the place he always stood these days. It was light outside, the sun high now, but darkness would again fall soon. He didn't mind this view, or being in the office. He was always in his office because he didn't have a family to go back to.

Mr. Parsons might have, but he didn't.

He watched the news. Two days until he proclaimed he'd capture and destroy every ULTRA. Of course, he knew that was a weighty goal. He knew he probably wouldn't achieve it. But it wasn't just about capturing and destroying every ULTRA. That was just a part of the plan.

The main thing he was lulling people into?

Being on side with the ULTRAbots.

Accepting them as peacekeepers of the world, without even batting an eyelid.

And if they did finally realize what was going on, it would already be too late.

He took another swig of his brandy. There was a tangible silence to the room other than the slight buzzing from the news. After Idris sadly passed away with a sudden heart attack in the corridor, there'd already been a loneliness about Mr. Parsons' existence.

It was a shame, what happened to Idris.

But Idris was an intelligent man. He knew something was amiss.

And for that, he'd had to pay the price.

He sat down and closed his eyes as he leaned back in his chair, and allowed himself to reminisce about just how perfectly the plan had unfolded so far.

He'd imprisoned the real Mr. Parsons three years ago. Taken on his identity with the last of his strength, while allowing his own strength to recharge. He'd... dealt with Mr. Parsons' family. But he'd spent most of his time inside this office, planning. Working.

He'd created the formula for the ULTRAbots. He pretended someone else had made the miraculous discovery. Really, they were born of his powers, cloned by his powers. Which meant that he was in total control of them. They didn't serve the interests of humanity. They didn't serve the interests of anyone but him.

The second stage of his plan was trickier. He'd spent years imprisoning ULTRAs in Area 64, testing on them, trying to use them to make the ULTRAbot program even stronger. But really, that was all just a ruse for the real plan, which he'd launched a week ago—an escape. A breakout, engineered to release some of the most warped, twisted

ULTRAs in existence. A justification for the launch of the ULTRAbots. ULTRAbots who were more powerful than those ULTRAs imprisoned. ULTRAbots that would defeat the ULTRAs.

He opened his eyes. Grabbed his iPad. Looked at the image he'd seen days ago when he spent his time beside Spark in his final seconds.

On there, he saw the blurred image of Glacies, sent directly from an ULTRAbot left for dead in the snow. Drawing Glacies out of hiding was just another part of the plan. Another way of lulling yet someone else into a false sense of security.

But he had another plan for Glacies. He had another contact who was very, very interested in making sure Glacies didn't walk this world for much longer.

He sipped some more of his brandy. It tasted acidic but beautiful on the back of his throat. If there were one thing he'd miss when his power finally returned to full strength—which was close—it was the bitter tang of a good brandy.

He'd miss parts of being Mr. Parsons. He'd miss elements of it.

But above anything, he was excited.

Excited to begin.

He thought some more about his contact. The one he'd saved from the bottom of those ruins. He'd told him about this plan. Not completely, of course. He'd told his contact that the plan was to break the ULTRAs out of Area 64, as well as training an army of ULTRAs to fight and destroy humanity.

But there was more to it than that, of course.

That was just another diversion. Another misdirection tactic to confuse the world, to confuse the likes of Glacies, as to what was really going on.

As for humanity, well. The plan wasn't to destroy them. Not all of them.

He had much more exciting plans lined up for humanity than that.

He stood up. As he walked across his office, past the abstract paintings, past the sculptures of great leaders, of battle re-enactments from the dawn of man to today, he felt his disguise slipping. He felt himself shedding his Mr. Parsons skin. The more he walked, the more he was certain he didn't need it anymore.

Especially not after the second piece of footage he'd seen on his iPad, direct from the eyes of the ULTRAbots.

Glacies had fallen right into his trap. Glacies and his entire army, in fact. Which included Orion.

He wasn't sure what to think about Orion's presence at first. It intimidated him a little. But then the more he considered it, the more he knew it just raised the stakes. Elevated the excitement.

He walked past more of his sculptures. Walked right toward the end one. The one he prided more than any.

His contact told him something else. Something terrifyingly brilliant. Information that he knew would be more powerful than anything else. Information that would kill Glacies.

Glacies was a mystery man no more.

Glacies was Kyle Peters, a seventeen-year-old from Staten Island.

And he was right where he wanted him to be.

He stopped. Stopped right opposite his most prized possession. He felt a smile twitching at his scarred lips. Saw a glimmer of a burned face in his reflection in the mirror at the other side of the room, half of it deformed by fire.

He raised his hands. Grabbed the object in front of him.

The helmet.

Saint's helmet.

His helmet.

And then he put it on his head. Pulled it over, felt it squeeze perfectly around his face, just like it had last eight long years ago.

He turned around. Looked right at himself in the mirror. Looked at the silver metal helmet. Looked at his real self.

His conquest wasn't over.

His conquest would never be over until he won.

Because he was Saint.

38

I f I'd known what was coming in the next hour—the hour that changed my entire life forever—then maybe I'd have thought twice about celebrating the victory at the ULTRAbot production facility.

I stood back in the room where... well, where the hell was this room anyway? You know the room I mean, though—the one where Orion took me to when I first met the rest of the Resistance. There was a much more positive attitude about the place now. Slice had a smile on his face. Stone seemed slightly drunk. Even Vortex seemed to be letting her hair down, having a laugh. As far as we all saw it, we'd struck a major blow into the heart of the ULTRAbot operation. That was a cause worth celebrating.

"You did good, kid," Stone said. He stumbled over to me, a narrow-eyed expression on his round, happy face. He patted me on the back with his heavy hand, something that made me wince. "Really came through back there. Wasn't so bad now, huh?"

I smiled. Nodded. "Thanks."

"Seriously," Vortex said, joining Stone by my side. She

smiled at me, her teeth just as yellow as ever. "I might be forced to admit I had you slightly wrong. Just slightly."

I tilted my head to one side. "Does that make me immune to the nightmares?"

She nudged me in the arm, and for a split second, her face turned into a skull-like monster, then flashed back to normal again. "Darling, nobody's immune to the nightmares."

I wanted to feel as happy and celebratory as the rest of the group. But there were a few things on my mind, a few things bothering me. First, Mr. Parsons. I'd found him back at the compound. We'd handed him over to the police, who dismissed him as a fraud. But I wasn't so sure. None of us were.

It didn't help that Mr. Parsons' wife hadn't been seen for months. Months, and nobody batted an eyelid.

What happened with Mr. Parsons? That was the question everyone was asking, silently behind the scenes.

I felt like everyone else in this room feared something awful was going on, related to my discovery. But they were so relieved about today's victory that they just didn't want to face up to the truth.

I saw Orion standing at the side of the room, back against the wall. Even though he was in here with us, he was away from everyone else. And I could hear him gasping for air.

"You okay?" I asked, walking up beside him.

He looked at me, his face still coated in that black mask, then looked away. "The fighting. It... It takes a lot out of me."

"I noticed," I said.

"What we did back there. It feels... It feels like a victory."

"I'd agree there."

"Then why aren't you happy?"

I thought I was doing a good job of covering up my fears. I'd kept my mask on for that reason. "My family. My friends.

They... They'll know something's wrong by now. They'll realize I'm missing. Mom'll be losing her mind."

Orion sighed. Shook his head. "So your bind to us isn't as strong as we thought."

"This isn't anything about my bind to you guys," I said, unable to temper my impatience. "I've just walked away from a life I've been living for years without even saying goodbye. You've gotta understand how tough that is, especially after... After what happened to Cassie."

Orion seemed to flinch when I said her name. "You're being sentimental. You cannot allow sentimentality to—"

"Maybe I am being sentimental," I said. A few of the other ULTRAs had noticed I'd raised my voice now. "And I accept I can't be who I was anymore. I accept I can't just go back to the way things were. But I can't just run away from them, either. Not like this."

Although I couldn't see his face, I could feel Orion looking at me with total disappointment. "Everybody here has made difficult decisions. Walked away from someone they love. Something they care about."

"And I'm not going to be another one of those people," I said.

I lifted my phone. Went to call Mom.

"You're putting them all at risk," Orion said. "You're putting everyone you've ever cared about in total risk. You might think you know how the forces against us work, but you don't. And you won't. Not until the day... The day everything's taken away from you without a choice. Not until you've no choice but to give up."

Orion's words spun around my mind. Although he hadn't really gone into depth about anything, that had to be the most open and honest he'd been with me since we'd met. I got the feeling his guard had dropped, and he'd shown me and everyone else a little more of himself than he liked.

"I appreciate it," I said. "What you're trying to do. How you're trying to look out for me. Protect me. But I can't just walk away from them. Maybe in time I will, but right now I've... There's just too much."

I pulled off my Glacies mask, for the first time, revealing my face to the ULTRAs around me.

"I've stood with you. I've done what you wanted me to do. Now I have to go."

Orion and the rest of the ULTRAs stared at me. The looks of elation had changed to disappointment. Total disappointment.

"Well I never," Stone said. "The kid really is a fraud."

Roadrunner tutted. "If he wants to go, let him go. We gave him a choice. He can live with it."

I saw Vortex snarling at me. The closer I looked into her dark pupils, the more I swore I saw tears building in her eyes.

"Good luck," I said. "Seriously. I mean it."

I got a few shrugs from the group. But mostly, that look of disappointment was all that met me.

I turned around. Closed my eyes. Pictured my street, my house.

"Don't—" Orion started.

It was too late.

I heard the bang, and I was outside my home.

I looked across the street. I had to go back inside. I had to speak to Mom and Dad. Had to say I'd just stayed the night at Avi's, and then tell Avi a different story, and then tell... Hell, I'd work it out.

My thoughts froze when I saw my house.

There was heat coming from it. I could smell smoke in the

air. And I could see it rising above, thick black smoke snaking into the sky.

"No," I muttered, staggering closer.

My house was in flames. Completely swamped in them. Outside, the fire department had closed the road and sprayed the hose up into the windows, through the doors.

I clenched my fists together. Bit my lip and stepped forward. Mom. Dad. I had to get in there. I had to help them. I had to save them.

I went to fly towards my house, mask still off, when I saw four people running out of the house.

They were holding on to a person each. When they ran out of the door, they planted them down on stretchers, which then sped them towards the ambulance a few meters away.

"No," I said, tears rolling down my cheeks.

I stood there, defenseless, and watched as the stretchers wheeled the two people away, away from the raging inferno, towards the back of the ambulance.

I watched as my life changed in front of me.

I watched as Mom and Dad disappeared into the back of that ambulance, disappeared behind the doors, and disappeared out of my life.

One of them, forever.

39

I sat on the chair in the hospital corridor and felt a sickening fear like I'd never felt before.

I saw people rushing past me. Saw nurses, patients, people coming to visit. Some of them looked at me, half-smiled at me, in that knowing way, like they knew I must be waiting for news. And then when they turned around, they whispered to one another. Speculated as to what must've happened. "That poor kid," I heard one of them say.

I didn't know how to feel about it. I didn't know whether to acknowledge these people.

I just felt sick.

The beeps around the hospital and the sounds of feet tapping against the solid corridor danced around my mind, taunting me. My mouth was dry, and I tasted a mixture of blood and sick. I could smell the medicinal tang hanging in the air, and that didn't help with my sickliness. I couldn't stop shaking. I just wanted this to be a bad dream. An awful dream.

A glimmer of hope lit up inside me. What if it was a dream? What if this was all some kind of creation by Vortex? A way of punishing me for turning my back on the Resistance?

I clutched on to that belief for seconds. Minutes. And then for an hour.

But the clock kept on ticking. The time didn't slow down. No illusion faded.

I was still waiting to find out whether my parents had survived the house fire.

Despite my banging headache, I couldn't rest my mind. I wanted to know who'd done this. I wanted to find whoever had done this and I wanted to destroy whoever had done this. I wondered whether it was the ULTRAbots, and they'd thought I was home and were targeting me. Or maybe it was an accident. Maybe it was another scrap between ULTRAbots and ULTRAs, and a flame had smashed right through my window.

No. It was too much of a coincidence. Someone was targeting me. Someone knew who I was and they were punishing me for my role in the fight.

I felt my jaw clenching harder as I sat there, guilt welling in my mind. If I'd stayed at home and not gone along with that stupid plan of Orion's, I could've been there when the flames hit my house. I could've stopped them. I could've frozen the flames and I could've got my parents out of there.

But I wasn't. I'd walked away because I felt some bullshit duty to Orion and the Resistance. But that wasn't me. That wasn't my fight. Hell, if anything, I should be with the humans and the ULTRAbots against the ULTRAs. 'Cause it was the errors of his generation of ULTRAs that had caused this mess in the first place. If the ULTRAs of his generation just behaved, just stuck to the rules, then maybe this would be a world where ULTRAs and humans co-existed after all.

But it wasn't. And I'd chosen Glacies over Kyle Peters. I'd chosen the powerful alias over the life I wanted to live.

I'd chosen this mess.

As I sat there, more footsteps passing by me, more people

looking at me with concern under the bright lights of this corridor, I started to wonder whether Orion had a point. It wasn't an easy thing to consider under the circumstances right now, but I couldn't help wondering.

Orion warned me what'd happen if I tried to live two lives. And I had. I'd tried to live as both Kyle Peters and as Glacies. And even though I'd chosen Glacies in the end, it was still too late. I'd been juggling existences for way too long.

Maybe that's what'd put my parents in the hospital. Maybe that's what'd destroyed my home. Not my decision to fight for the ULTRAs, but how damned long it took me to make that decision.

It didn't matter now, though. It didn't matter at all because there wasn't a thing I could do about it.

My parents were in hospital. They were injured. Severely injured.

And I was sat here waiting for the news.

I felt my phone vibrate against my leg. When I lifted it, I saw a message from Ellicia. I didn't want to open it. Didn't want to see what she had to say. Not because I didn't want her here— I wanted her here right now more than anything. But because I was scared. Scared of accepting that there were other people in my life, too. Other people who I could be putting in danger.

I'd already stared into my burning house as my parents were dragged out on stretchers. I'd already sat on this hospital chair once now. I didn't want that to happen again.

I opened the message anyway.

Saw the news. Coming hospital now. Hope you're okay. Missed you last night. x

I noticed right then that I had thirty missed calls, some from Ellicia, some from Damon and some from Avi. I felt guilty. Guilty because they didn't know I was okay. For all they knew, I was in one of those hospital beds right now, fighting for my life.

Or worse.

I opened up a message and went to reply the same thing to each of them.

I'm okay. Mom and Dad not so good. Need some privacy now. Will speak later.

I sent the message, fully aware it came across cold, but not really caring at all right now.

I got an instant reply from all three of them.

Thank God, bro. From Avi.

Ring me ASAP From Damon.

Love you x From Ellicia.

I wiped a tear from my eye and swallowed a lump in my throat as I put my phone away. I wanted to reply to them. To speak to all of them. But I couldn't. I just couldn't.

When I looked up from my phone, I saw a dark-haired woman standing over me in a nurse's outfit.

She gave me that half-smile. That tilted half smile that made my insides turn to mush. "Kyle Peters?"

"My mom," I said. "My—my dad. They're okay. Right?"

She held that half smile for a few seconds. Held it for the longest few seconds I'd ever known.

"Your dad's fine. He's hurt, few nasty burns, but he's fine. Should be able to walk outta this place in a day or two."

I felt relief crash through my body. I shook even harder as the adrenaline settled in my muscles. "And—and Mom?"

That half-smile again. Only this time, there was a darkness to it. More of a tilt to it.

"My—my mom," I said. My heart raced. Butterflies battled around my stomach. "Please. Please tell me she's okay."

And then, the words I'd been dreading hearing my entire life.

The words that changed everything.

"I'm sorry, Kyle. I'm really sorry. Your mom didn't make it."

40

I stood by my dad's hospital bed and held his hand.

I still couldn't take in the news I'd received half an hour ago.

Dad was in a private room off the main ward. Sure, I could still hear the footsteps tapping along the corridor outside, the beeping of the hospital equipment in the other rooms, the chatter and laughter of staff, patients, everyone.

But there was nothing in this room. Nothing.

I just held on to my dad's hand.

My dad held on to my hand.

We were silent.

My dad looked in bad shape. There was a scar on his head. He had an oxygen mask over his mouth. He also had some sore-looking burns down his right side, but the doctor was convinced that he was going to be okay and out in a few days. And I wanted to be happy about that. Of course I did. I'm sure Dad wanted to be happy and relieved about it too.

But how could we feel anything at all when we'd just learned that Mom hadn't made it?

What were we going to do without Mom?

Every time I thought about the last time I'd seen her—being wheeled out of my burning house and into the back of that ambulance—the more I wanted to break down and cry. I should've been there. I should've saved her. I should've stopped this. Instead, I'd been away fighting a battle that wasn't even mine.

Mom had died. Mom had died, and I'd let her die.

Dad coughed, spluttering a little. I held on to his hand. As much as I wanted to be far, far away from everyone, from anyone, I knew I had to be here for him right now. I knew I had to be by his side. Mom was his rock. They'd been high school sweethearts right from the first day they'd met. They'd always been by each other's sides, through good and through bad.

Mom was gone.

Mom was gone, forever.

It still hadn't sunk in properly. Still hadn't hit me. I felt lost, in a dazed trance that I wasn't sure I'd ever break out of.

"It's okay," I said, holding Dad's hand tighter. "I'm here. I'm not going anywhere."

Dad pulled aside his oxygen mask. Coughed some more.

"You need to keep that on," I said, trying to pull it back over his mouth.

He raised a hand. Shot a glance that told me not to even bother trying to reapply the mask. He didn't want it. He'd made his decision.

I stood there by his bed longer. I thought of Mom as I'd known her. Always smiling. Always trying to do right by Dad, by me, by everyone. Even after Cassie died, Mom was the one who brought the family back to its feet. She was the one who held Dad together—as much as she could.

And now she was gone.

My heart pounded. I couldn't breathe properly. I needed to get out of here. I needed to get away. I needed to—

"It's okay," I said, tightening my hand harder around Dad's. I tasted salt on my lips from the tears I'd cried when the news was first broke to me. I expected them to flow. Expected myself to break down in hysterics.

But all I felt was emptiness. All I felt was a hole widening in my life.

"I'm here," I said.

"You can't be."

I looked at Dad. What did he mean by that? I had to be here. It was my duty to be here. "I'm not going anywhere."

"You have a responsibility," Dad said, his breath wheezy. "A responsibility to the people. A responsibility to everyone. You can't be here."

A responsibility to people? To everyone?

"What do you—"

"The CCTV footage. At the garage. You don't have to pretend anymore, son."

My stomach dropped out of my body. I looked my dad in the eyes and he looked back at me.

"You know," I said.

"I'm not that stupid," he said. "Coulda figured it out without the CCTV."

My hand loosened. I backed away from the bed. "You can't know. Nobody can—"

"Well I do," he said. His voice had dropped to a whisper now. "I've seen what you can do. I've seen what you're capable of. I've seen you look evil in the eye and take it down all because you care about people."

I still couldn't believe it. I felt like I was in some horrible nightmare. Mom was gone. Dad knew I was an ULTRA.

"I'm sorry," I said.

"You don't have anything to apologize for."

"I could've saved Mom. If I'd been there, I could've—"

"No," Dad said. He coughed after he spoke. Tears built up. "No, you can't believe that. None of us can believe that. Believing that's the shortcut to insanity. For now you... you just have to focus on moving forward. We both do."

I sat by the side of Dad's bed. My head ached with a combination of *everything* that'd happened. It was hard to believe a life could change so dramatically in a matter of seconds, and mine had changed several times already today. "I don't know what to do anymore," I said, finally, exasperated and desperate.

Dad reached over. Took my hand in his. He shuffled around so he was looking right into my eyes. "You are what you are. And you have a responsibility to embrace what you are. It might not feel nice. It might not feel good. But look around you. Look at what's happened. Not just to Mom, but to others. To people all around the world. You have the capability to put a change to that. *You* have it in you to stop it. And you're just gonna stick around here and feel sorry for yourself?"

I was surprised with how hard Dad was talking to me, especially after we'd both learned that Mom was gone. But I supposed grief had a way of affecting everyone differently. "I'm scared."

"Well that's just tough, son," Dad said. "That's just damned tough. We're all scared. We're all scared to grow up. To leave home. To get a house of our own. We're all scared about bills to pay. About retirement. About putting food on the table for our kids. We're all scared about somethin'. But we find a way. Because it's what we have to do. It's what *you* have to do. Right now."

I wasn't sure I'd ever felt more sick, more awful, more horrified and gripped by shock than I did right now.

But Dad's words spoke to me. They spoke to the part of my soul that wanted to give up. The part of my soul that wanted to walk away from my life as an ULTRA for good.

"You go and do what you have to do, son. Do it for Mom. Do it for me. Do it for everyone."

I swallowed a lump in my throat. I stood. Leaned over and kissed my dad on the cheek.

"I'll come back for you," I said, tears streaming down my face now.

My dad half-smiled at me, his eyes red and bloodshot. "I know you will." His voice was shaky, on the verge of breaking completely.

I wanted to stay here by his side forever. I didn't want to leave him again.

But I knew I had a responsibility.

I had a duty.

I had to grow up, right now.

I walked away from Dad's bed. I looked around at the CCTV in the room, focused on it. Then I snapped the camera away from its stand using nothing more than the power of thought, honed and powerful with all the grief and anger and rage and sorrow I felt inside.

"I'll come back for you," I repeated.

"I love you," Dad said.

I sniffed. Felt more tears on my lips. "I love you too."

I closed my eyes and focused on the one place I needed to be right now. Because whether I liked it or not, I knew what I had to do.

I knew what I had to *be*.

"I love you," I said, the picture of Mom in my mind, standing by the front door, smiling as I walked off to see Damon and Avi, like she always did no matter how old I'd got. "I love you."

I took a deep breath.

Disappeared.

I knew what I had to do.

41

I sat in Avi's bedroom and prepared to say the hardest things I'd said in my life so far.

There was a rare silence to Avi's house. No video games on his massive new television, which he'd afforded with his part-time job at McDonalds. No smell of pizza in the air, which was particularly weird. Just me, him, Damon and Ellicia, all sat in his bedroom, all quiet.

I knew why they were quiet. They were quiet because of me. After all, what did you say to someone who'd just lost their mom? Whose dad was seriously hurt in hospital?

I didn't know what I'd say if I were in their shoes. There probably wasn't anything *to* say.

But there was something I did need to say. Something I knew exactly how to say.

It wasn't going to be easy. But I was going to have to do it. For the good of my friends, for the good of my girlfriend.

"I just... I don't know how to tell you this," I said, my voice cracking, my mind still not able to process the events of the day —of what had happened to my mom.

"In your own time," Ellicia said. She grabbed my cold hands

between her warm fingers. Smiled at me, that made me feel at ease inside. I wished I could sit there and hold her hand forever. I wished I could look into her eyes for the rest of my life. I wished I could be Kyle Peters.

But I couldn't. I couldn't be Kyle Peters because it was too dangerous to be Kyle Peters.

"My dad and I," I said, trying to get the words out. "When he gets outta hospital. Which shouldn't be too far off. We're going... we're going away for a while."

I heard the silence of the room change. A shift in understanding, as Damon, Avi, and Ellicia all looked at me differently.

"Away where?" Damon asked.

I kept my focus on Ellicia. I hated having to tell this lie. I hated having to do this at all. But what else could I do? What other choice did I have? "Just across the country. For a while. Staying with family over in California."

"California?" Avi asked, exasperation in his voice. "Man, can I come with you?"

I could tell he was trying to be light and humorous. But there was no humor about the room anymore. Ellicia's rosy cheeks had gone pale. She saw what this was. I was leaving her. I was leaving home.

But there were two things she didn't know.

One, I wasn't going to California at all.

Two, where I was going, I wasn't coming back. Ever.

I stood up. I didn't want to make this linger any longer than I had to. I wasn't good with goodbyes. Plus, my friends and girlfriend didn't know exactly what kind of a goodbye this really was. They'd see soon that I'd lied. They'd see Dad was still home and start to ask questions. But I'd cross that bridge. I'd cross that bridge when the time was right. "Anyway. Should get back to Dad. Need to get planning this trip."

"You're leaving, like, soon?" Damon asked.

I hadn't expected Damon to be the one asking the questions, the one looking so... upset, about all this. I was stupid for that, though. I'd known Damon a long time. He was my best friend. And I was turning my back on him. Walking away.

For the good of humanity, sure. And for the good of Damon himself, too. Maybe one day he'd realize that. Maybe when I was on my deathbed, I could tell him everything—who I was, what I'd done. I could picture him, seventy years old, awe and amazement in his eyes as he learned all about everything his best friend had done, everything he was capable of.

For now, though, that was a long time away.

Right now, I had to do those things I wanted him to be in awe of.

I walked up to Avi. Gave him a hug, and tried to stop the tears building.

And then I stepped over to Damon. He looked at me with those big, watery eyes, like an upset puppy.

"Gonna miss you, man."

I stepped towards him and he gave me a big, tight bear hug. This time, I couldn't keep the tears in.

"I'll miss you too," I said.

As we held on to one another, I thought about the times Damon had my back over the years. The times he'd picked me up when the bullying at school got rough. The times he'd made me smile when I didn't think it was possible.

"You've made me what I am," I whispered.

Damon pulled away. Wiped his eyes. "Huh?"

"Nothing," I said, smiling. "It... it doesn't matter."

Damon flicked me in the arm. "You keep in touch with us, yeah?"

"'Course I will," I said, knowing damn well that was a lie. It was too dangerous to keep in touch with them. I saw that clearly now. "I'll wanna know all about Avi's dating stories."

"And I'll wanna know all 'bout them California girls!" Avi said, laughing. "That book's down to a 4.3 on Goodreads now. But man, it's still fire."

I laughed in return. It felt good to laugh. Made me feel a little better again.

I walked away from Damon and Avi and stood opposite Ellicia.

She hadn't said a word since I'd said I was leaving. She'd just stood there, pale-faced, a glassy-eyed look about her.

Where did I start? What did I possibly say? I had the girl of my dreams. I had her, as me, Kyle Peters, and I was walking away from her.

What was I doing?

What the hell was I—

"You go be where you need to be right now," she said, softly. "I'll wait for you. I promise."

I felt a knot tightening in my stomach as I leaned towards Ellicia, as I kissed her soft, velvety lips.

"I love you, Kyle," she whispered.

My heart fluttered with both warmth and sorrow. "I love you too."

We kissed again. And then I walked away. Walked across Avi's room to the bedroom door. I saw all his posters. His Halo posters. His stacks of video games. Games I'd played in here time and time again. I saw old pizza boxes. I saw that damned online dating guide he claimed was so effective.

I saw all of it as if for the first time, even though I knew it was for the last time.

"See you soon, man," Damon said.

I forced a smile, but I couldn't turn and look at them. Not again. Not the way the tears were flowing down my face.

"See you soon," I whispered.

Then I walked away, out of Avi's room, away from my best friends for the very final time.

Away from my life for the very last time.

I undid the top button of my shirt. Felt the Glacies outfit rubbing against my skin.

There was someone else I had to be right now.

Another life I had to live.

Forever.

42

Bowler tried not to feel too pessimistic. Pessimism was a fool's game.

But right now, optimism was a liar's game.

They were losing a war before it had even begun.

He stood at the front of the secret room where he and the other members of the Resistance always met. He'd stood here so many times over the last few weeks, the last few months, the last few years. But now was the first time he'd seen such a look of defeat across the faces of those who were supposed to be fighters. Such a stare of disillusionment, frustration, with the current situation.

Still, it was his job to make the plans. To galvanize the troops. He just wasn't sure how much fight was left in them, let alone in himself.

"The ULTRAbots are much more resilient than we might've assumed," he said, hating the echo of his own voice as it boomed around the room. "We destroyed one of their facilities, but the government responded violently by ramping up production at another of their facilities over the Pacific Ocean. We also believe that several new facilities have been erected. The truth is, the ULTRAbots are getting stronger, they're growing in number, and the ULTRAs are decreasing."

A blank stare from Stone, a look of worry from Aqua. Even Vortex looked concerned, lost in a real-life nightmare for a change.

"Then what exactly's the plan?" Slice asked.

"There's only one thing we can do," Bowler said. "Launch another attack on an ULTRAbot facility. Reduce their numbers."

"And you really think that's gonna work?" Ember snapped.

Bowler shrugged. He wasn't sure what to say. In truth, no. He didn't think it was going to work. But what other option did he have? "It's all we've got."

"It's like whack-a-mole," Aqua interrupted. "We take one down, another will step up. And then they'll just keep on stepping up until... well, until whatever."

"But we have to fight until whatever," Bowler said. "Because that's just who we are—"

"No," Slice said.

Bowler looked right at Slice. So too did a few of the others.

Slice shook his head. Pushed his glasses up the bridge of his long nose. "No, that's not who we are. It's who *you* are, but it's not who we are."

"We are one—"

"Enough of the shit, *Orion*," Slice snapped. "We've lost this. It's over. There's nothing else fighting's gonna do for us. Our best shot right now? Hide. Get far, far away from each other and hide. 'Cause there's one day left, in case you hadn't noticed. One day, then Mr. Parsons' big ULTRA-cleansing plan comes to an end. If we can just hide until that day passes, then maybe. Just maybe."

"The ULTRAbots aren't gonna just stop operating after tomorrow," Aqua said, impatiently. "That was just a ruse to get people on side. There's no real plans to ditch the ULTRAbots. Not now the government has the perfect security system."

"Then maybe we shouldn't hide at all," Slice said. "Maybe we should just throw the towel in right now. Hand ourselves in. Hell, maybe they'll even go easier on us. Whatever we do's better than staying here and walking into another suicide mission."

Bowler shook his head as Slice turned away. "Don't do this."

"I'm sick of following every command you give us," Slice shouted. "The fact is, there isn't a resistance. There never was a resistance. There was just you and those dreams of yours. It's over, Bowler. Orion. Or whatever you want me to call you. See it for what it is. It's over, and there's not a thing you or anyone on this planet can do about it."

"That's not true."

Bowler looked to the right. He wasn't sure who the voice came from. Not at first.

Not until he saw Glacies standing at the opposite side of the room.

Everyone turned and looked at him, open-mouthed.

"How did you..." Bowler started.

"We are going to fight," Glacies said, walking past the ULTRAs in the middle of the room. "We're going to fight because if we don't fight, every last ULTRA is going to die. And then worse. Something's gonna happen to the humans, too. We know it's not Mr. Parsons really behind this. We know something weird's going on. We don't know *what* exactly yet, but we know something's wrong, and if we don't act fast, we'll be finding out the truth very soon. And we can't just stand around and let it happen."

Stone tutted. Rolled his eyes. A few pieces of rock sprouted around his fists as he tightened them. "And why in the hell should we listen to a weak little runaway?"

"Because I'm here right now," Glacies said, his voice getting stronger, more confident. "I'm here because I've seen what happens when I try taking the other route. When I give up on who I really am. We can try hiding, sure. We can try living our life like we're normal. But we're not normal. And we need to use that. We have a duty to this planet to use that."

Bowler saw a few of the ULTRAs' faces turning. None of them protesting. Even Slice was holding his ground.

Glacies kept on walking in front of them. "This is our lives. This is who we are. We don't give up. We keep on fighting. Because we're ULTRAs, and that's what ULTRAs do."

A pause. A silence.

Then, "He's right."

Bowler looked across the room. Saw that it was Vortex who'd spoken. She had a smile on her face now, like she was enjoying all this way too much.

"I don't particularly like the guy's methods. But he is right. We stand together. We take their dreams. And if we have to, we fall crying into the night."

Glacies stepped in front of Vortex. Nodded. She stepped forward and joined him.

"You don't have to do this," Glacies said. "Not if you don't want to. But please. Think about the world. Think about all the people out there, just trying to live normal lives. Think about the ULTRAs like us. Hunted down by the governments. Put through unthinkable pain. Think about them. And only then, decide you don't want to join us."

There was no movement for a while. To the point that Bowler thought this was it. Just Glacies and Vortex.

"Hell, I'm with the kid."

Stone stepped forward. Then too did Aqua and Ember, and Roadrunner. And soon it was just Slice standing where he'd stood all along, cutting a lonely figure.

"Please," Glacies said. "Join us."

He hesitated. And then he sighed. "If I'm going to join you, I at least want to hear your plan."

It was at that point that Glacies turned and looked Bowler right in his eyes.

"We do what Bowler said. We take the fight to the ULTRA-bots. We take down every last one, just like they want to do to us. But above anything, there's something else we need to do. Something way more important."

"And what's that?" Slice asked.

"We need to find out who their leader really is. And we need to take them down."

43

"**A**re you ready?" I shouted.

I saw the ULTRAs behind me, hovering over the ULTRAbot compound in the middle of the Pacific Ocean, waiting to attack.

"Ready," they shouted.

"Good," I said. "Then we attack."

I flew down towards the ULTRAbot compound beneath us. Immediately, I felt the bullets from the drones blasting around me, trying to fire into me. I dodged them. Focused as intently as I could and jumped around them, out of their way.

I ran up to one of the drones. Grabbed the back of it. Latched on to it. And then I held my breath and teleported it opposite another of the drones, sending both of them erupting in a burst of flames.

I looked back. The rest of the ULTRAs were all engaged in fighting of their own. We'd spent a day planning, deliberating, and decided to take a different approach attacking this facility, going for the hammer-blow instead of the sneakiness of the previous attack. We figured it'd be a good way to surprise the ULTRAbots.

Besides, we were together. We were focused.

And when we were focused, we were strong.

I heard a door opening over on my left. When I looked, I saw a crowd of ULTRAbots all stepping out in that mechanical way they always did, all looking right up at me, at the rest of the Resistance.

"Watch out!" I shouted.

And then as the ULTRAbots lifted their guns, I pounded right into them with force.

The explosion was enough to blast away a good twenty, thirty of the ULTRAbots upon contact. I felt the flames surrounding me. Tasted smoke in the air. My neck ached from the contact with the ground, but I didn't have time to mope about it, didn't have time to worry.

I readjusted my footing and turned to the ULTRAbots opposite me.

They were surrounding me. Hundreds of them. All standing around, all with weapons raised, all getting ready to fire.

"Bring it on," I said.

The first ULTRAbot to make a move was one on my left.

It pulled the trigger and fired right at me.

Only I wasn't there when the bullet reached my position.

I punched it back. Knocked it into the ULTRAbots behind it. And then as the gunfire rattled all around me, explosion after explosion erupting, I kept on moving, jumping, shifting around and knocking down as many ULTRAbots as I could. I heard shouting from the rest of the ULTRAs fighting alongside me. I saw flashes in the sky. I knew this time, the plan was for Stone to go inside and disable the ULTRAbots. And I hoped he hurried. I was doing okay right now, but I couldn't hold off an army like this forever.

I felt a heavy fist crack right across my face.

It knocked me to the ground. Sent me flying into the concrete.

More ULTRAbots pointed their guns at me as I lay there, blood in my mouth, wounded.

Then, they fired.

I shifted out of their way again with my dwindling strength. I hovered above them, then rained down a ball of ice right on top of them, freezing them instantly.

I crashed down into them. Sent their frozen bodies shattering all over the place.

But still there were hundreds of these things, swarming around me like flies around cattle.

I kept on punching back. Throwing punches and fighting with all I had. But I could feel my powers weakening the more punches I took in turn. I could feel my head spinning. One slip and they'd have me. One slip and everything would be over.

As I fought back, the ULTRAbots getting stronger and stronger around me, I thought of Ellicia, Damon, Avi. I thought about Dad. He knew who I was. And he'd told me what I had to do.

"You go and do what you have to do, son. Do it for Mom. Do it for me. Do it for everyone."

I thought about Mom. The last time I'd seen her, smiling at me as I left the house for what seemed like such a normal day compared to now. How I'd never see her again.

And I felt my chest tightening. I felt my punches back getting stronger.

"You go and do what you have to do, son. Do it for Mom. Do it for me. Do it for everyone."

In my mind, I saw the look of pain in Dad's eyes as I walked away from him in his hardest moment. As his own son turned his back on him to be here—where he needed to be. This damned place. This damned—

Another smack, right across my face.

I fell. There was nothing I could do to shake myself free of my current situation. I lay back on the ground and watched hazily as the ULTRAbots lifted their rifles, as they pointed them at me.

I closed my tearful eyes. Braced myself for the blast.

I'd be with Mom soon.

I'd be with Mom.

And then I heard a shout.

I opened my eyes. Above, I saw Stone jumping into the middle of the ULTRAbot ring. They turned their attention away from me to him.

He was completely covered in rock. He punched the ULTRAbots out of the way, one punch taking down about five of them at a time.

"Go!" he shouted.

I watched as he fought off more of the ULTRAbots, all of their attention on him now. I held my breath. Tried to fix my face, which ached like mad. Focused on healing. Focused on getting away from here. On getting inside the ULTRAbot facility.

But all I could see was Stone.

All I could think about was him standing there in the middle of this ring of ever-advancing ULTRAbots, surrounded.

"I'll hold 'em off instead. You go and disable 'em. Quick!"

I closed my eyes. Clenched my teeth together.

Teleported myself just outside the ULTRAbot facility, being careful not to teleport through the door to avoid being fried—a security measure that Roadrunner warned me about from her scouting missions.

I looked back at the ring of ULTRAbots I'd stood in the middle of just moments ago. I could see Stone in there, still punching back, still fighting. But the punches were getting weaker. He wasn't knocking as many of them back. Not anymore.

I wanted him to be okay. He'd put his life on the line for me.

But I knew what I needed to do if I wanted to save him.

I ran inside the compound. Jumped past the bullets of the ULTRAbots standing guard right in front of the main door, just like the last compound. I opened up wormholes, portals, whatever the hell they were with all the strength I had. Threw the ULTRAbots through them, as heavy as they were, and tossed them somewhere in the ocean far away.

And then I ran down the stairs.

When I stepped inside the compound where the ULTRAbots were produced, I noticed something different in there.

The ULTRAbots weren't in their chambers. They weren't sleeping, ready to be awoken.

They were standing.

Hundreds of them. Thousands of them. All waiting to fire.

I looked over at that red button. The de-activation button. I could try getting over there. But I didn't have much—

Gunshots. Gunshots blasted past me, crashed into the concrete wall beside me.

I moved back up the stairs and fell. Smacked my head onto the concrete. As I lay there, I heard the ULTRAbots progressing, getting ever closer.

I looked over at that red button as the footsteps marched nearer. I thought about Stone. About what he'd done for me. Putting everything on the line for me.

Then I thought of the fire.

Thought of Mom. Of Dad. Of Ellicia.

I couldn't give up.

I couldn't ever give up.

The ULTRAbots stepped around the corner. Hundreds of

them. I could hear them walking into the compound from the main entrance now, too. I was surrounded. We'd lost.

They all lifted their guns.

For a moment, I thought I saw smiles on their faces.

"Too late," I gasped.

And then I used every inch of power in my body to press down that red button with nothing more than my mind.

I saw the ULTRAbots shake. Saw them lower their weapons. And then electricity sparked from them. Their eyes went wonky. Their mouths opened and closed, opened and closed.

They fell to the floor, all of them, shaking as electricity sparked from their bodies.

Then, there was a massive bang. A massive bang followed by an eruption of smoke.

Then, the ULTRAbots were still.

I took a moment to appreciate the silence. To recover from the falls I'd had. I'd come close. So close. But I'd done it. We'd all done it. We'd shut down another facility.

We had to keep going.

I got up. Ran past a ton of fallen ULTRAbots and outside the main door.

When I saw the mound of ULTRAbots lying in front of me, saw the morose looks on the faces of Aqua and Vortex, I knew there was bad news.

"Stone," I said. I walked over to the ULTRAbots. Tossed them away, two at a time.

"It's over, Glacies," Orion said, struggling for air. The battles were still taking it out of him. He put a hand on my shoulder. "He's gone."

"No!" I shouted. I kept on throwing the ULTRAbots aside. Kept on tossing them away. I couldn't give up on Stone. He'd not given up on me. He'd sacrificed everything for me.

I was about to toss another ULTRAbot out of the way when I saw Stone lying right beneath me.

His eyes were closed. His body was still. There were no stones on his body. Just bruises. Lots of bruises.

"No," I said, backing away. "I can't—"

"We have to leave," Orion said, defeat in his voice despite another victory. "I'm sorry. For all of this. But we have to—"

"Damn. You really ain't a soppy bunch, are ya?"

I looked down and saw Stone staring angrily up at us.

"Stone!" Aqua shouted. She went down to join him, as did others, as he pulled his way from the mound of ULTRAbots.

"You're alive," I said.

Stone raised his eyebrows. "'Course I'm alive. Just wanted to see how you guys'd handle my funeral. As it happens, not well at all. Gotta improve on that."

I felt myself laughing at Stone. I couldn't believe I was laughing, especially after everything that'd happened. But I was. I was Glacies, and I'd conquered this place. All of us had conquered this place. We were the Resistance. We were a team. And we weren't going to stop at anything.

"Wait," Aqua said.

I turned to look at her. So too did everyone else. "What's up?"

She was looking at a screen. "You... you need to see this."

I walked over to Aqua. And as I walked, I saw the rest of the ULTRAs look up at me in turn, then back down at the screen. I knew right then this was something else about me. More bad news.

I considered all the options. All the horrible options.

What I found was completely different.

On the screen, I saw Mr. Parsons. Not the real one. But the government one. The one taking his form.

He was talking. Lecturing a crowd on the day of his deadline.

And on the screen, there was a photo of me.

Not me as Glacies. But me as *me*.

Kyle Peters.

"We all know this young man," Mr. Parsons said, "but by a very different face and a very different name."

"No," I said, feeling my world melt around me.

"This young man is the leader of the ULTRAs. This young man is the one individual standing between peace and war."

"No!" I started to run, to get away, but Orion grabbed me, stopped me from moving.

I looked into Mr. Parsons' eyes as he spoke. I knew what he was going to say. I knew what the words were going to be. I knew my entire world was going to fall apart, again.

"This young man is Kyle Peters. Glacies."

I heard gasps from the crowd. I imagined Ellicia's parents watching the news in disbelief. I imagined the nurses tending to my dad suddenly looking at him with fear. I imagined it all, and I felt everything caving in.

"Mr. Peters," Mr. Parsons said, looking into the camera now. "I know you're out there, somewhere, engaging in some kind of brutal fight against humanity with that band of bloodthirsty misfits of yours. It's time for you to come back to reality. To see how much you really care. To complete your..." He smiled, and for the first time, I thought I saw another face behind this avatar of a man. "To complete your impossible mission."

My stomach sank.

Every muscle in my body dropped.

I heard voices. I heard words. I knew the ULTRAs around me were trying to talk, trying to calm me down.

But I couldn't. Not after what Mr. Parsons just said.

My impossible mission.

"Ellicia," I said.

I pushed Orion and Vortex away. Rushed over the fallen ULTRAbots to the edge of the manmade island in the middle of the ocean.

"What?" Orion asked. "What is this?"

"My impossible mission," I said. "Mission Impossible. It was our—our first proper date."

Aqua frowned. "I don't understand."

"Ellicia!" I said, as the horrifying reality of my situation welled up. "He's—he's got Ellicia."

44

I flew towards Ellicia's house without a thought of the potential repercussions.

The air was thick and humid considering it was winter. There was no snow on the ground anymore, like it had all just melted away with all the battles between ULTRAbots and ULTRAs, and with the news that had broken just minutes ago.

The news identifying me, Kyle Peters, as Glacies.

The news exposing me to the entire planet.

I landed outside Ellicia's house. I didn't know where else to go. I knew the rest of the Resistance had tried to stop me leaving, but that was worthless. Sure, I was Glacies, and I had responsibilities and duties to the ULTRAs above anyone. I got that now.

But I wasn't losing anyone else.

I wasn't losing Ellicia.

I held my breath and camouflaged as I looked down the pathway leading to Ellicia's house. I looked around for signs of life. The road was too quiet. I felt like people were watching me, even though they couldn't possibly see me.

I held my breath again and teleported myself inside the house.

I stood in Ellicia's bedroom. My heart sank when I saw she wasn't there. I looked around for her. Looked under the bed, inside the wardrobe. I checked the other rooms. The bathroom, her parents' bedrooms, downstairs in the living room and dining room.

But it was worthless. Ellicia was gone.

I stood there and looked around. A bitter taste filled my mouth. I'd let someone down, again. Here I was, being played, all because I'd tried to live two lives. I regretted ever meeting Ellicia. I regretted ever getting attached to anyone. The damage had already been done. There was nothing else I could do.

I knew right then that there was something I could do, though. Something I could try, anyway.

Mr. Parsons, or whoever was pretending to be Mr. Parsons. He knew about Ellicia. What he'd said about my "impossible mission," that couldn't just be a coincidence.

He was trying to draw me to Ellicia. One way or another, he wanted me here.

I looked around and saw shadows creeping closer to the house.

I stood still. Completely still. I wasn't sure who was outside, but I could guess. The army. ULTRAbots. All of them closing in, surrounding me.

I pictured the footage of this siege unfolding on the news. I pictured Ellicia watching it, hand over her mouth, unable to believe or accept that her boyfriend was the most powerful ULTRA in existence. That he'd lied to her about his identity for so, so long.

I realized then that there was no going back now. No matter what, life would never be the same. Not now Damon knew. Not now Ellicia knew. Not now everyone knew.

I'd tried to live two lives. Kyle Peters and Glacies. Now, I'd been left without a choice, just like Orion told me I would be all along.

I was Glacies.

I'd live as Glacies, and I'd die as Glacies.

But one thing was for sure.

I wasn't letting anyone else I cared about get hurt.

I closed my eyes. Focused my rage as the footsteps outside got closer. I needed to go. I needed to get away before they closed in completely.

And then I heard something upstairs.

It was faint. Very faint. And I swore I'd checked upstairs thoroughly.

But then I heard it again.

A kick. A cry.

Ellicia.

I flew up the stairs, no regard for the surrounding army outside. I searched every room for Ellicia. Again, I looked under the beds, in the wardrobes, in the...

When I looked in the bathroom, I saw her.

Ellicia was lying in her bathtub. She was tied at the ankles and the wrists. She had tape over her mouth and was crying out underneath it.

"It's... It's okay," I said, stepping into the bathroom toward her. "I'm here now—"

I felt myself bump into an invisible wall.

I tried to push past it, to push through into the bathroom. But something was stopping me. I lifted my hands. Banged against it. Still, I couldn't get through.

It was then that I felt that horrible sensation like someone was watching me.

"Hello, Kyle."

When I heard the voice behind me, I didn't want to believe it at first. It couldn't be possible. It couldn't be true.

But as I turned around, the sickliness growing deep in the pit of my stomach, I knew it added up. I knew it was real. I knew that everything had been building towards this impossibility all along.

"Good to see you again."

Dark hair.

Silver armor.

A wry smile across his skinny face.

"You can't be..."

"Well, I am. I am."

Daniel Septer was alive.

Nycto was alive.

"I think it's about time we caught up properly, don't you?"

45

"**W**ell? I thought you'd be a little happier to see me."

I stared across the upstairs hallway of Ellicia's house into the eyes of Daniel Septer. My mouth was dry. I couldn't speak, couldn't think. Every muscle in my body was tense as if the ice I could blast from my hands had coated me, wrapped me in its clutches. Outside, I could hear the muffled advance of the approaching soldiers. Behind me, the faint whimper of Ellicia as she lay tied up in that bathtub.

Daniel Septer—Nycto—who I'd fought.

Daniel Septer—Nycto—whose reign of terror I'd ended six months ago.

Daniel Septer—Nycto—standing opposite me.

"How you finding my new look, anyway?" Daniel asked. He stepped closer to me, his silver armor not glowing as strongly as it used to. One-half of his face was covered in shadow. But as he moved towards me, I saw it clearly.

It was burned. Burned on the scalp, right down across his left eye. His neck was covered in burns, too. I knew it was Daniel just from the good half of his face. But as I looked at the wrinkled mess of skin that the bad half had become, I couldn't help feeling guilty.

"You certainly made your mark, Kyle," Daniel said, grinning. Only one-half of his face moved. "I mean, I'm sure you wanted more than to wound me. I guess that's the whole reason you threw me down into Krakatoa in the first place. Left me beneath the lava. But hey." He extended his arms and his grin. "Here I am. Here we are. What a wonderful reunion."

"How?"

I knew how pathetic I sounded spouting out that single word. But it was all I could say. Nycto was supposed to be gone. I was supposed to have dealt with him.

So how was he here right now, standing opposite me, in Ellicia's house?

Daniel chuckled. He leaned against the wall. I could still feel the force field he'd created between the hallway and the bathroom pushing against my back like two magnets opposing. "Hmm. Now, how I got out is a long story. I mean it. Considering a book deal, but I hear the self-publishing route's just as good these days. Anyway, how I got here doesn't matter. How I got out of that volcano... well, let's just say you underestimated my strength."

"I buried you in that lava. I froze it and brought Krakatoa down."

"You thought you did," Daniel said, a slight hint of laughter to his every word. "I mean, I can see why you thought you caused those series of eruptions. I can see why you thought that was your power and not mine. But anyway. You were so busy trying to save humanity that you didn't even notice me escape."

I cast my mind back to Krakatoa's eruption. I'd put all my focus into saving those islands from the eruptions that I hadn't even considered Daniel might've escaped.

"I mean, you hurt me," Daniel said, stepping closer. "You

didn't just give my body scars. You gave my powers scars. And that upset me. A lot."

I felt a tingling sensation at the back of my neck and knew Daniel was inches away with his powers.

I saw the flames grow from his palms as he moved closer. He was so close that I could smell his sour breath. He looked into my eyes with something that resembled bitterness. Anger. "But I'm here now. I'm here, and you're here. And I've got you all to myself. Not to mention her."

He looked over my shoulder and I knew what he was referring to. "Leave her out of this."

"Oh, it's way, way too late for that. I mean, the world knows who you are. The world knows Kyle Peters is Glacies. How does that feel? How does it feel being the most wanted ULTRA in existence?"

"Stop this."

Daniel laughed. "All this time and you still haven't changed. Not a bit. Not like me. No, I realized the error of my ways before. I realized I had the wrong approach. I couldn't take the world alone. I needed ULTRAs. ULTRAs on my side. ULTRAs who'd been screwed by the world. I needed them, and only then could I destroy the vermin of humanity. Only then could I create a beautiful new world order."

"You haven't changed," I said. "You're still a psychopath."

Daniel smiled. Shrugged. "Maybe I am. Maybe I'm not. But I'm powerful. More powerful than ever before. And that's the main thing."

I heard shouting outside. I knew whatever happened here, I had to make a decision. I couldn't just let everything come crashing down around me at the hands of Nycto.

"The ULTRAbots," I said. "They... they were yours. All along."

Daniel frowned. "No. Oh, God no. I wish they were."

"You're lying."

"Why would I lie, Kyle? Why on earth would I lie when I have a whole army of ULTRAs behind me?"

My mind raced for answers. The escaped ULTRAs from Area 64. The ones attacking the people. They were Nycto's.

But then, if they were Nycto's, then who was behind the ULTRAbots?

Who was Mr. Parsons?

"Let's just say I made a very powerful government friend with a very similar interest to me. I gave him your identity, as well as the identity of other ULTRAs who I knew were never going to turn to my cause, and he gave me some ULTRAs of my own."

I shook my head. "It doesn't make sense."

"Maybe not to small minds," Daniel said. "But this isn't a world for small minds. Not anymore. This is a world for thinkers. For—"

"Mr. Parsons. The man behind the ULTRAbots. He isn't who you think he is. He's playing you. Playing you like he played me."

Daniel's smile didn't falter. Not for a moment. "It doesn't matter really, does it? I'll destroy him too, when the time comes. Right now though, the ULTRAbots are providing a necessary distraction. We will strike. When the time is right. But anyway. We have more important matters at hand right now. Like your first inauguration speech."

I felt sickness creep over my body. "What do you mean?"

Daniel smiled. "I'd advise you keep an eye on your girl in future."

I frowned. Turned around.

Ellicia was gone.

She'd vanished.

I went to run into the bathroom, to look for her.

Then I stopped.

"Where is she?" I barked.

Daniel put his helmet on his head, became the full embodiment of Nycto. Stretched out his arms. "Why don't you come and find out?"

Anger filled my body. Rage dripped through my system. I wasn't letting him win. Not again.

"I'd like to keep it peaceful, ideally," Nycto said. "But I understand if—"

I didn't listen to another word Nycto said.

I flew at him.

Hard.

I didn't make contact with him, though. I didn't make contact with him at all.

I heard a bang. Saw a flash of light.

When my eyes cleared, a sense of dread overwhelmed me.

"Welcome," Nycto said. "To your inauguration."

I was hovering above Times Square, above thousands and thousands of people, all of them staring up at me, taking photographs, watching.

Many of them holding photographs of me, Kyle Peters. Of my family. Many of them shouting, spitting, booing.

There weren't just people, though. Beside Nycto, there was a massive line of ULTRAs hovering in the air. Nycto's ULTRAs. Nycto's army. All waiting to fight.

I wanted to get away. To leave. But I had to save Ellicia. I had to stop...

Something was different.

A breeze hit my face.

When I lifted my hand, I felt pure skin.

I wasn't wearing my Glacies mask.

Nycto had it in his hand.

He lifted it up. Smiled. "Time to say goodbye to the good old days," he said.

He tore the Glacies mask in two.

I stared down, my live image on the screens of Times Square, my identity known to the angry world, and I knew right then that life would never be the same.

If I survived to live another day.

46

"Come on, Glacies. Or should I call you Kyle? Come down. Fight me. Show the whole world who you really are."

Nycto's voice spun around my head. I floated there above Times Square, my face and my name all around me in the glow of the afternoon sun. I pictured Damon and Avi seeing the news. I pictured my teachers from school. The government. Families, people I knew, people I used to know.

All of them knew who I was now. All of them saw exactly what I was.

I wasn't Kyle Peters to them anymore.

I was Glacies.

"If you're so powerful, come down here. Fight me. Save Ellicia."

I swallowed a lump in my throat as I looked down into the middle of Times Square. Nycto was hovering part way off the ground. Behind him, his crowd of ULTRAs braced for battle. And beneath them, Ellicia, dangling off the edge of a window. I knew I'd have to pass Nycto if I wanted to save Ellicia. I knew

I'd have to fight him, causing destruction in the process, turning more and more people against me, against ULTRAs.

I knew I'd have to embrace Glacies if I wanted to save the girl Kyle Peters loved.

"Come down here and show your true face to the world."

"You're more talkative than I remember," I shouted.

Nycto had his silver armor mask on, but I could picture the smile on his face from up here. "And you're less action than I remember."

"That's what happens," I shouted, "when you learn to care about people. When you learn to give a damn about the world."

A pause. I heard my voice echo through the massive speakers in Times Square. Some of the crowd were beginning to disappear, to run away. Icy sleet started to fall. I knew they were braced for an inevitable battle; an unstoppable showdown that would claim more and more lives.

But as I hovered there, exposed, without my mask, I felt an understanding growing inside. Yes, the world knew who I was now. They knew what I was capable of. The strength I had. Yes, I was going to be hated by some. I was going to be hunted by many.

But I had a chance.

A chance to speak.

A chance to do the right thing.

"I don't want to fight," I shouted.

My voice reverberated down the sides of the buildings. I saw some of the ULTRAs turning their heads, looking right at me. Whispers grew amongst the crowd of people below.

I hovered there, looked around at as many people and ULTRAs as I could. "We've fought enough. Humans. ULTRAs. All of us. We've fought enough already."

"It's all your fault!" someone screamed.

"You aren't the only ones who've lost in this," I shouted

back. "I... I've lost too. I lost my sister eight years ago to the Great Blast. I lost my mom—my mom, just yesterday." My voice stuttered when I spoke those words. "I've lost my life. My own life as a seventeen-year-old dork. I've lost it all, and there's nothing I can do to change that."

More silence grew amongst the crowd. Nycto kept on floating there, his army behind him, waiting for his call.

I drifted closer to the ground. This made some more people run away, disappear. "Now isn't the time to fight," I shouted. "There's a great threat heading our way. And when I say 'our', I don't just mean ULTRAs. I mean ULTRAs and people. Because we're the same thing. Different in what we can do, sure. But I wasn't so different to any of you down there. Not long ago."

On the massive screen on the side of the 20 Times Square building, I saw a woman's eyes filling with tears. A few people looking at me with... with something like understanding.

"You might think we are the enemy. And I'm not denying that some of us have bad intentions." I cast a glance at Nycto. "But the good ULTRAs, the ULTRAs that have fought for you behind the scenes for so many years, we're not the bad guys. We want to protect you. To live amongst you. To help you."

"Then why do you blow our cities up?" a man cried. More protest erupted on the ground below.

"The ULTRAbots," I said. "You might think they are the saviors. You might think they are the protectors. But there's something you should know. Something you should understand. Mr. Parsons. The man claiming to be fighting for your cause. He isn't who he says he is."

Many confused glances spread around the crowd like a fire.

"I found the real Mr. Parsons locked away in one of the ULTRAbot production facilities. He'd been trapped in there for months. He had no idea about the ULTRAbot program. About anything that was going on. So we have to ask the question together, all of us. Who is behind the ULTRAbots? And when they get us ULTRAs out of the way, what do they really want?"

"Liar!" someone called.

"No, he's telling the truth."

I wasn't sure where the voice came from. Not at first.

And then, as my eyes adjusted to the pixelated screen, I saw exactly who it was. Right on cue.

The real Mr. Parsons walked through the crowd. Cameras snapped at him. He'd had a shave and a haircut, but he was clearly emaciated and withered. He stood in the middle of the crowd and looked everyone in the eye.

Even Nycto and his army froze in confusion, in puzzlement.

Mr. Parsons cleared his throat. Scratched at the back of his neck. "I don't know who's pretending to be me, taking my form. But I know one thing. Glacies saved me from that cell. From that personal hell. If it wasn't for him, for his—his people, I dunno if I'd ever have got out."

He nodded at me. And I felt the sincerity in his words. Sheer confusion gripped Times Square. It was the final day of Mr. Parsons' deadline. The day he claimed every ULTRA would be wiped off the face of the earth. Every single one.

"We need to unite," I said. "All of us. We need to demand whoever is in government shows their real face. Because we won't stand for this. We won't take any more loss. Any more fighting. Not anymore."

I saw some of the rival ULTRAs nodding. And then, by my side, I saw that Orion—in his Bowler gear—and the rest of the Resistance had joined me. They nodded at me, some still looking a little pissed after my walkout earlier, Stone in particular. But they were by my side. They were with me now.

"Got your back, kid," Stone said. "We must be crazy, but we've got your back."

I floated above Times Square with the Resistance behind me. Beneath me, Nycto and his armies, who were clearly wavering in their opinions. Under them, humanity, holding its breath, waiting for something to happen, something momentous.

"Nycto," I called.

He turned around. Looked right up at me, at the Resistance.

"We don't have to fight. We shouldn't fight. Not anymore."

He was silent. The rest of the ULTRAs were silent. The humans on the streets below covered their mouths with their hands.

"Attack," Nycto shouted.

I held my breath and braced for the impact of Nycto's ULTRAs. I clapped my hands, sparked up a fistful of ice. Stone took on his rocky form. Aqua sprayed water below. We braced ourselves. Prepared for war.

But something happened.

Or, rather, something *didn't* happen.

Nycto's ULTRAs were still. Completely still. All of them were looking up at us with uncertainty in their eyes. With understanding in their eyes.

"You heard me," Nycto barked, turning around to face them. "Attack!"

"No," one of the ULTRAs—a ginger guy with thick black smoke spewing from his hands—said.

A pause between them. Then, "What do you mean, 'no'?"

"We mean no," another ULTRA said. And then before I knew it, all of the ULTRAs were flying past Nycto, rising up towards the Resistance, floating by our side.

All of us, all one hundred, two hundred of us, looked down at Nycto, as did the cameras. He cut a lonely, dejected figure. Part of me was happy to see him like that.

But part of me wanted him to join me. Because I knew if I

could win him over, he could be an asset. Not a friend, but an asset. Someone who could help.

Nycto took off his helmet. Threw it down to the ground below. More people gasped as his burned face was revealed. His good eye was bloodshot. His jaw shook.

He was silent. For a moment, he was silent.

"Never mind," he said. "I'll just have to take you myself."

Balls of flames grew rapidly from his hands.

"But first..."

He raised his arms. Pointed them down at Ellicia.

"No!" I cried.

He went to fire.

And then I heard it.

An explosion. An explosion bigger than any I'd ever heard, ripping through the air on my right.

Instead of the brightness I expected to see that always accompanied an explosion, I saw darkness. A cloud of sheer darkness heading my way.

A cloud I'd seen before in my life. I'd seen it on television. I'd seen it firsthand. But a cloud that couldn't be possible.

Because Saint was gone. Saint was long gone and buried.

Wasn't he?

I saw the darkness getting thicker.

Saw the day turn to night.

"No," I heard Orion whisper. "No."

I knew from those words that my worst fears were true.

My nightmares were realized.

My nightmare was Saint.

And he was coming right towards me and the remaining ULTRAs, with a million-strong army of ULTRAbots behind him.

47

I watched as the black cloud grew closer and I felt a shiver moving up my spine.

The ULTRAs around me were silent, both those of the Resistance and those who'd been behind Nycto originally. Even Nycto was quiet, watching as the sheer darkness edged nearer, the thousands upon thousands upon thousands of ULTRAbots along with it.

I could hear a faint humming growing gradually louder. The more I thought about it, the more certain I was I'd heard that same humming all those years ago as an eight-year-old kid, on the day I'd watched my sister die.

The humming that terrorized humanity.

The humming that came from Saint.

It was here again.

I squinted into the middle of the darkness and saw him moving closer.

It was strange, seeing someone so talked about through recent history that they were pretty much a myth. It was like I was in the middle of an inescapable dream, and this ULTRA rapidly gaining on me and the rest of the ULTRAs around me weren't really here. I felt like I could open my eyes and snap back to reality; a reality without Saint.

But there was no denying that silver armor. There was no denying that skin-tingling hum.

And there was no denying the confidence that he floated with just meters away.

Saint was back. Saint was right here.

And he had an army of ULTRAbots behind him.

He lifted his hands. Below, it was easy to forget there were so many humans, all watching the drama above unfold. They were dumbstruck. Stunned to silence.

I felt my teeth chatter. Beside me, I saw the terrified looks on the faces of my fellow ULTRAs—ULTRAs of both sides.

I wanted to fight. I wanted to strike back at Saint right away. I wanted to finish him before he even had the chance to start.

But it was true what people said about him; people who'd lived in the old days. There was something about him that hypnotized you. Something that filled you with a twisted kind of awe, even if you were in fear of him.

Which I was. Everyone was.

He brought his hands together and he started clapping.

"Bravo," he said, his voice echoing through a silent Times Square. Even the cabs and cars had ground to a halt, keeping their hands off the horns.

Saint kept on clapping, his focus on me, on Nycto. "I mean, it didn't work out exactly as I wanted. Ideally, you would've killed one another right here. Destroyed each other. Met the little deadline Mr. Parsons set. But never mind. We'll be finished with you soon."

I saw the ULTRAbots edging closer. There were so many of them, they blocked out the light from the sky.

"How?" Orion shouted. "How are..."

"Nice to see you again," Saint said. The bottom half of his

mask was cracked slightly, revealing a smile. "Just so we're clear, there's no hard feeling between the two of us, right? I mean, we're two sides of a coin, really. The two originals. The birth of the legend. We shouldn't be standing opposite one another right now."

"I killed you," Orion said. As he spoke, I heard mumbling below. More people realizing that Bowler—the Man in the Bowler Hat—was, in fact, Orion.

Some people even started to flee as they realized just how catastrophic all these revelations could be.

"You wounded me," Saint said. "Critically. But I've been putting my downtime to good use. Building up to this day. This... very special day. This historical day—"

"Let me join you!"

I heard Nycto's voice echo across Times Square. He drifted over towards Saint, towards the ULTRAbots, who all turned their attention to him.

Saint glanced at Nycto like he was nothing more than an annoying fly. "And you are?"

"Nycto," he said, pulling off his helmet and revealing his charred face, like it proved his identity somehow. "I—I believe in you. I created Nycto in your image. To achieve *your* goals. Well, we differ. I think you like humans better than I do, but we can work on that. And it was you, wasn't it? It was you who let me break the ULTRAs out of Area 64. You did that for me. Didn't you?"

Saint let out a cackle. Moved backward, the laughter so biting that it was electric. "You really believed you were important to me? You really believed you were anything other than a pawn in my game?"

I saw the redness spread across Daniel's face as Saint continued laughing at him, laughing at him like bullies had laughed at him all his life. And I felt something weird. Sympathy. Because Saint was a much bigger deal than Nycto. Saint was the real deal.

"I'm insulted, frankly," Saint said, regaining his composure. "Insulted that you would offend my image with that cheap waste of a costume."

"It's not cheap."

"You failed," Saint shouted. "One chance to take control of the world, and you failed at the hands of another kid. How does that make you feel?"

Nycto—Daniel Septer—turned and looked at me. I swore I saw a tear roll down his cheek.

"Anyway," Saint said. "I've just about had enough of you for one day, little fly."

He lifted his hand and swatted gently to the right.

Nycto went crashing out of sight. He flew through buildings, explosions following in his wake. Debris fell and rained on the people below.

I stared stunned at the spot where Nycto had been tossed away like garbage. Nycto was strong. He was almost my match. Almost.

And Saint had flicked him away like a gnat.

"We have more important matters at hand than pesky idolators," Saint said.

Now, he looked right at me.

"Your little game. All of you. It's over now. If I were you, I'd get out of here. Fast."

I clenched my jaw. Felt my hands turn to ice.

"Kyle," Orion said.

"We'll never run," I shouted.

Saint smiled. Tilted his head to one side. The ULTRAbots behind him kept their trance-like focus on me, on the rest of the Resistance. "Really, kid? Is that the game you want to play?"

"It's not a game," I said, feeling the anger building inside.

The anger at the person who'd killed my sister. The person who'd killed her, standing right opposite me. "And you aren't going to get what you want. Not this time."

Saint shifted, suddenly just inches in front of me. So close that I was staring right into the dark eyes behind his helmet.

"You're wrong," he said. "I will get what I want. I will get what I started. Total rule over humanity. Only now I have the ULTRAbots on side, well... I don't need ULTRAs anymore."

He lifted his hand and shot a blast of electricity behind me.

I heard a scream. A shout of pain.

When I turned, I saw Aqua falling to the ground below.

Her body was tingling with electricity. Vortex and Stone hurried down after her. Slice held his ground, his face growing redder, the anger building in his eyes. "You—you killed—"

Another blast of electricity flew from Saint's hand.

It slammed into Slice's chest.

Knocked the consciousness from his eyes.

Sent him falling to the ground below, down below with Aqua, like a swatted fly.

I felt sick. Tasted vomit in my mouth as my heart pounded. I heard the cries of the ULTRAs. The panic. Saw some of them disappearing. Some of them fleeing. Everything collapsing. Everything falling apart.

I looked back at Saint. He had his hand raised. Electricity tingled from his fingertips.

He smiled.

"Time to dance, Kyle Peters," he said.

He shot a bolt of electricity right at me.

I dodged the shot. I didn't have much strength in me, but I swung out of the way of it.

And then the ULTRAbots flew towards me. Sent shots firing at the Resistance, firing at the ULTRAs of Nycto's side. I saw the panic on the streets below as the battle of confusion raged in the skies. As buildings exploded, as explosions erupted all down the streets. I saw chaos everywhere. Explosions. Madness. Panic.

And then I saw Ellicia.

She was still hanging on to the edge of that window ledge. Looking right up at me as the world around her fell apart.

"Better hurry, Kyle," Saint bellowed. "Wouldn't want to let the girl fall now, would we?"

I wanted to stop Saint. I wanted to fight him as the ULTRA-bots and the ULTRAs all fired at one another, scrapped in the air, as more ULTRAs fell from the sky like the snow New York had been expecting, down onto the panicked streets.

But then I saw Saint raise his hand.

Point at the building Ellicia was dangling from.

Fire.

I flew down towards her. Hopped through the sky. Because as much as I knew I was going to have to be Glacies now, I had to save Ellicia. I couldn't just let her fall.

I saw her lose her grip. Saw her drop down towards the street below. I stretched out my hand to fire some ice at her, or to ease her fall using my telekinesis, but then an ULTRAbot grabbed onto my arm, pointed a gun at my chest.

I batted free of it. Shifted behind it and fired its own weapon into its robotic skull.

I didn't have long. More of the ULTRAbots surrounded me.

I flew down toward Ellicia as her fall grew faster. I felt time around me slow down as I saw the chaos, the flames, the destruction.

I clenched my teeth into my lips so hard I tasted blood. Tried to shoot ice, to use telekinesis all over again.

Still, my powers failed me.

Still, Ellicia fell.

I saw her just meters from the ground. Then just one meter.

Then half a meter. And as the humming of Saint echoed above me, I thought about Cassie. About Mom. About everyone I'd lost all 'cause of this.

I felt the ULTRAbots closing in as Ellicia fell closer to the ground.

I felt my time running out completely.

And then I let out a cry.

A blast of power left my chest when I cried. I felt cold light slam out of my body, shattering all the ULTRAbots around me.

And as I screamed, I saw Ellicia was still falling in slow motion.

Millimeters from the ground.

The sidewalk drifting up to meet her inevitable fall.

I kept on screaming, and I felt myself getting closer to Ellicia, but not close enough.

I kept on screaming, and I saw Saint above, embroiled in a battle with the people I'd fought with, with the ULTRAs Nycto had fought with, tossing them aside like they were nothing.

I kept on screaming...

And I saw Ellicia hit the ground.

Then, darkness.

48

I felt the darkness surround me as Ellicia hit the ground.

But something stopped her. Something deep inside me. I forced myself towards her. Then I forced a wormhole to appear in the ground beneath her. And in the total silence, despite all the destruction around us, despite everything in the world that I loved falling apart, I rushed into that wormhole with her and disappeared into the nothingness.

While I was in there, I held on to Ellicia. It was dark. Jet black. I could hear screams and see images from my youth—being held underwater, muffled voices above me. Cassie's face as the Great Blast ripped through the world.

"It's okay," I whispered to Ellicia as we disappeared into this endless dark oblivion. It felt like behind us, the world was still there. Like the Battle of Times Square was still in full force. But we were getting further and further away from it, closer and closer to the one true place we needed to be.

Somewhere at peace.

We landed. I felt the ground smack into my side as Ellicia landed onto me. Her mouth was still covered by duct tape. Tears rolled down her cheeks.

I looked around at our surroundings. Mountains. Trees. A little village in the distance, where people tended to their cattle. One of the islands I'd rescued when I'd destroyed Krakatoa. One of the places where I'd earned the trust and respect of the natives.

Which is exactly where Ellicia needed to be right now.

I put my hands on her arms. She flinched as I moved towards her, her eyes wide and confused. I knew then why. She knew who I was. She knew I was Glacies. And she was afraid.

"It's me, Ellicia," I said, as if that was gonna do any good. "Please. It's me, Kyle. Let me take the tape off."

She hesitated. Held herself back. But this time, as I moved my hand to the tape, she let me pull it away gently.

"That's it," I said. "You're okay now—"

I felt a crack across my face. "Get away from me!"

I watched Ellicia run away. I saw the fear in her eyes, and it made my heart sink. Here she was, the girl I loved, the girl I'd spent so much of my life trying to convince to love me back, treading through the tall grass in a place she didn't know where she was to get as far away from me as she possibly could.

"Wait," I called.

Ellicia fell. Her knees landed in the dirt. I caught up with her. Sat by her side. And as I did, she punched at me. Kicked at me. Spat at me and threw soil at me. And I let her. I let her do all this without repelling the pain because I deserved to feel this way. For keeping my true identity a secret for so long. For trying to live two lives.

If I hadn't lived two lives, Ellicia wouldn't be in this kind of danger. She wouldn't have had to go through what she'd just gone through.

Eventually, she stopped kicking and punching. I held her arms. "Please," I said. "Just hear me out. Just hear me out..."

She wrapped her arms around me and cried before I could

even speak. I put my hands on her warm back and I cried too. She was burning up, so I made my hands a little cooler as we stood there in the Asian sun, some of the villagers down below starting to take notice of us.

She backed away. Looked at my Glacies bodysuit. Then back at my face. She stroked the suit, then moved her hand up to my face and stroked that, as if it was a mask. "You're him," she said. "You're really him."

I shrugged. Forced a smile. "Sorry to disappoint!"

I realized my attempt at humor was lame and well out of place. But it was something. It was an interaction between us.

As much as I didn't want to admit it, Ellicia and I weren't going to be interacting much after today.

"Why didn't you...?"

"Tell you? Because I was afraid. Partly, anyway. Another part... well, I didn't want to accept that I had to be Glacies. Because believe me when I tell you that Glacies doesn't want anything bad to fall upon the world. *I* don't want anything bad to fall upon the world."

"You saved me," Ellicia said. Her breathing was speeding up, and her cheeks were whitening. "From the party. The school party. And—and then from Daniel when he was in my house. You saved me."

I nodded. "I did what I had to do to keep you safe."

Ellicia shook her head. Staggered backward. "God. Oh, God."

"I'm sorry," I said. "I'm sorry I was never honest with you. In all truth... it's because of what being honest meant. For us."

She looked me in the eye again. "What does being honest mean for us?"

I opened my mouth and felt my Adam's apple quivering as I prepared to say the words I knew I had to. "We can't see each other. Not for a long time. It's... it's not safe. For you. For you or

Damon or Avi or Dad. All of you need to lay low. Until it's over. Until I've dealt with Saint."

She stood there shaking her head, like she was taking it all in. "When you said goodbye. When you told me you and your dad were going away. You were saying *goodbye* then. I knew it. Weren't you?"

I looked at the grassy ground and nodded just the once.

"Kyle I... I can't just let you walk away. Not now."

"You have to," I said.

"I won't let you."

"And I won't let you follow me."

She looked at me like she didn't recognize me. And that was the hardest thing to take at all.

"There's a village down there. Helpful people. They helped me get back to strength after my battle with Nycto. After I saved their village and their island from Krakatoa. They owe me a favor. I'll get your family here. You'll be safe here. And then when the world's safe for you again, I'll be back. I promise."

I turned around and wiped a tear from my face. I couldn't have the conversation anymore.

"And when will that be?" Ellicia asked.

I opened my mouth. But I knew I couldn't answer. Saint and Orion's war had raged for three years and had been raging behind the scenes even longer as the pair planned their next moves, unbeknownst to the other. I wanted to lie to Ellicia. To tell her I wouldn't be long. But I was done with dishonesty. "I really don't know."

I stood there for a few seconds. Breathed in the warm air. If I cleared my mind enough, I could convince myself I was still just Kyle Peters. That I didn't have ULTRA responsibilities.

But I did. It was who I was. And I had to accept them.

I felt a hand on my arm.

I didn't want to look into Ellicia's eyes again because doing so was painful. But still, I turned around.

She smiled at me now. I saw that look she'd given me when I'd seen her at the soccer stadium before all the madness happened with the gunmen. I saw the way she'd looked at me before we'd known each other properly, and I felt like we were learning to know each other all over again.

"Let me come with you to wherever you're going," she said.

I wanted to say yes. I was touched that she'd asked.

But I knew it wasn't possible.

"I can't do that, Ellicia."

She tightened her grip on my arm. "I want to. If I want to, you have to—"

"The world's not safe," I said, sternly. "And it's not going to be safe as long as Saint is out there. The world needs me. People need me. Even if they don't think they do... they do."

She lowered her head. I knew right then that I'd broken her argument. She was usually so good at getting back at me. For the first time since we'd got together, I'd left Ellicia speechless.

"You're safe here. And as long as I'm alive, you'll be safe. That's a promise. But right now... I need to go, Ellicia. I need to fight. I'm so sorry."

She looked up at me. I expected her to argue back.

Instead, she pulled me close and pressed her tear-tasting lips against mine.

She backed off. I could smell the sweetness on her breath, and felt that icy sensation up the back of my neck when her eyes met mine. "Come back for me. Please."

I felt my teeth chattering and pretended it was the cold. "I will," I said, holding eye contact with Ellicia, precious eye contact.

"Promise?" she asked.

I stepped away. Looked back over the mountains, at the

island. "I'll get your family here. You'll be safe. And I'll be... I'll be back for you."

"Promise, Kyle?"

I cleared my throat. "Promise."

I stood there for seconds, maybe minutes, not saying anything. Just waiting. Waiting for the right moment. Waiting for the moment to disappear.

"Bye, Kyle," Ellicia said.

I turned back. Looked into her eyes. Her gorgeous blue eyes. Her chocolate brown hair. Her beautiful face.

I felt another tear hit the top of my lip, and I knew, staring into Ellicia's eyes, that right now was the time.

"Goodbye," I said.

I held my breath. Embraced all the upset, all the pain, inside.

And then I disappeared.

Ellicia vanished in front of me.

But she'd never vanish from my mind.

Never.

49

I never thought I'd fly above the world as it ended beneath my feet.

The morning sky was dark. It was always dark these days. Especially dark when Saint was on his way to a city, or when he'd just visited a city.

It was just after Christmas, but there hadn't really been a Christmas this year. People were too terrified. Too afraid. Some of them imprisoned, as Saint led his trail of chaos and destruction from city to city.

He told the world that he was doing it for their own good. That the ULTRAbots would keep them safe, just as he'd told the world the very same thing when he'd masqueraded as Mr. Parsons. But I saw what this was. Everyone saw what this was.

Saint was taking over the world. He was breaking city after city, country after country, away from civilization, imprisoning everyone in their own little cell.

And he was moving fast.

"Are you ready for the next move?"

I heard Orion's voice beside me. I turned to him. Looked at his dark, masked face.

I looked back down at the swathes of ULTRAbots below as we floated high in the sky. It was like watching an army of ants move between nests. If I fell right now, I could walk on the backs of them.

But there were too many to deal with. Way too many to deal with alone.

I looked past Orion. Looked at Stone. At Vortex. At Roadrunner and Ember, and at the one hundred and something ULTRAs who'd stood by Nycto's side just weeks ago. We were together now. *We* were the Resistance.

Or at least what was left of it.

"We have a war to fight," Orion said. "We have to be in it together. Completely. All of us. For better or for worse."

The loss of Aqua and Slice left a bitter taste in my mouth. They'd been cast aside needlessly. Two pointless losses. Two good ULTRAs. Losses that would haunt us all forever.

I knew there would be more losses. We all knew there would be more losses.

But I was determined to keep those losses as low as I possibly could.

I wasn't going to give up. I wasn't going to let their deaths be for nothing. I wasn't pretending anymore.

I *was* Kyle Peters. Not Glacies. Not some false identity.

I *was* Kyle Peters, and I was an ULTRA.

This was my life, whether I liked it or not.

"Kyle?" Orion asked.

I looked back at Orion again. Then at the rest of the ULTRA Resistance. I saw them all looking at me. Waiting for me to give the call. To say the word.

Then I looked back down at the ULTRAbots below.

"I'm ready," I said.

WANT MORE FROM MATT BLAKE?

The third book in The Last Hero series, Battle of the ULTRAs, is now available to buy.

If you want to be notified when Matt Blake's next novel in The Last Hero series is released, please sign up for the mailing list by going to: http://mattblakeauthor.com/newsletter Your email address will never be shared and you can unsubscribe at any time.

Word-of-mouth and reviews are crucial to any author's success. If you enjoyed this book, please leave a review. Even just a couple of lines sharing your thoughts on the story would be a fantastic help for other readers.

mattblakeauthor.com
mattblake@mattblakeauthor.com

Made in the USA
Coppell, TX
17 October 2021